CIARAN

Dunskey Castle 11

JANE STAIN

janestain.com

Druid Magic (Tavish, Seumas, and Tomas)

Celtic Druids (Time of the Celts-Picts-Druids)

Druid Dagger (Leif, Taran, Luag)

Meehall

Baltair

As Cherise Kelley:

Dog Aliens (a cuddly dog story with a happy ending)

High School Substitute Teacher's Guide

FOREWORD

To answer some of the questions you may have when you read Ciaran:

***

Branding cattle:

"In earlier centuries, much of the livestock trade had been in the hands of monks, but once cattle became symbols of wealth among warring clans, there was constant threat of pillage, often leading to skirmishes in which men were killed.

"In 1603, eighty men died in Glenfruin when the MacGregors were attacked while trying to lead away a large herd [which had been stolen from the MacGregors, who were reclaiming it].

"To end this, authorities brought in a range of strict controls and branding methods, and strictures on markets and butchering. These measures helped stave off a minor civil war based around livestock."

The Doric Columns, "The Drovers"

http://www.mcjazz.f2s.com/Drovers.htm

These toy iron soldiers give you an idea about the size of a halberd, the out of focus weapon held by the fighter on the left. Halberds are also called war axes.

On the next page is a close shot of a halberd (also called **halbard**, **halbert** or **Swiss voulge**), a two-handed pole weapon that came to prominent use during the 14th and 15th centuries. The word *halberd* may come from the German words *Halm* (staff), and *Barte* (axe). In modern-day German, the weapon is called a **Hellebarde**.

Troops   that   used   the   weapon   are
called **halberdiers**.

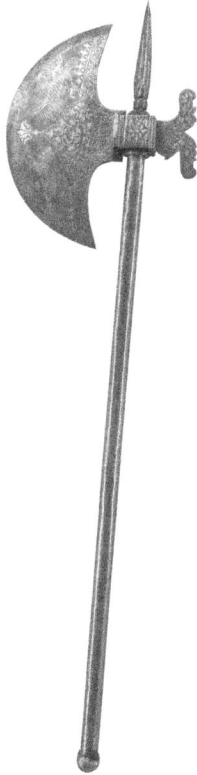

The halberd consists of an axe blade topped with

a spike mounted on a long shaft. It always has a hook or thorn on the back side of the axe blade for grappling mounted combatants.[1] It is very similar to certain forms of the voulge in design and usage. The halberd was usually 1.5 to 1.8 metres (5 to 6 feet) long.[2]

The word has also been used to describe a weapon of the Early Bronze Age in Western Europe. This consisted of a blade mounted on a pole at a right angle.[3] [4] A very similar weapon, the dagger-axe, from Bronze Age China, has also been called "halberd" in English.

***

Regarding the Cameron fortress in this story:

Ewen "Eoghainn MacAilein" Cameron, XIII Chief of Clan Cameron, built the highly disputed Tor Castle (said to have been on Clan Mackintosh lands) in the early 16th century. Tor Castle would remain the seat of the Camerons of Lochiel until demolished by his great-great-great grandson, Sir Ewen Cameron.

Sir Ewen Cameron wanted a "more convenient" house, further removed from Clan Mackintosh. He built Achnacarry Castle (Scottish Gaelic: Achadh na Cairidh) around 1655 in a strategic position on the isthmus between Loch Lochy and Loch Arkaig.

One of the few remaining descriptions relate that Lochiel's seat was "a large house, all built of fir-planks, the handsomest of that kind in Britain."

Others portrayed old Achnacarry as "a man's home, with the feel and look of a grand hunting lodge amidst the West Highlands."

https://en.wikipedia.org/wiki/Achnacarry

Ciaran winced as his distant MacGregor cousin from the future haggled with the breech-wearing farmer for an apple wagon and two horses. Eoin had riches nary a highlander dared dream about, so why was he being so stingy? Ciaran had seen him spend more on a night's food and drink, albeit for the lot of them.

As the deal was clinched and Eoin's kilt swayed on his climb up onto the driver's seat, Ciaran met eyes with his contemporary MacGregor cousin Baltair. "Obviously," they said to each other with their faces, "if Eoin goes intae the future, then we're gang along."

But Eoin spoke up, loud enough for the farmer to

hear as well. "One o' ye wull need tae bide and work off the rest o' the cost."

Baltair's jaw dropped.

Eoin rolled his eyes. "Nay forevermore, ainly for a day."

Ciaran opened his mouth to protest.

But Eoin made as if to whip the horses into action and leave without the both of them.

Ciaran instantly shut his mouth.

But Baltair gave Ciaran a look that said the two of them were solid against Eoin, no matter what else happened.

And Ciaran acknowledged it with a firm but tiny nod.

""Tis settled," said Eoin imperiously from the seat of the wagon. "I wull ainly be taking one o' ye, sae draw straws." He picked some straw cushioning out of one of the apple crates, put two ends even, then covered the rest of the two pieces of straw with his fist, holding it out. As they came close enough to choose, he softly whispered, "The true task o' whosoe'er remains behind is tae make certain nay one goes intae the woods tae see why the wagon hasna come oot, ye ken?"

Ciaran focused on choosing his straw, then compared it to Baltair's.

Instead of pleasure at winning the draw, the implications of what his cousin had just said rolled through Ciaran's mind. He and Eoin were taking the wagon and leaving Baltair behind for a day. Eoin didn't want anyone going into the woods to investigate why the wagon hadn't come out.

There was only one explanation: Ciaran and Eoin were going to time travel.

Pleasure at last dawned in his mind. Aware he was failing to hide it, Ciaran climbed up into the wagon next to Eoin, lowering his head a wee bit to mumble to Baltair, "'Tis ainly a day. Ye wull gae the next time."

Eoin lashed the horses into action, driving the wagon forward until they had passed through the apple orchard and gone up the mountain a bit.

Now that Ciaran got a good look at it, he thought this small Rowan woods was a likely place for them to time travel. There was no road into it, and the wood was dark and chilly, making him snug his jerkin more tightly around his chest and his kilt more tightly around his knees.

So this was it. Ciaran was going to be a time traveler like Eoin, Meehall, and Sarah, the woman Meehall would marry. Like Nadia and Ellie, Sarah's two friends who Ciaran and Baltair had helped rescue a few days past.

Ciaran had known about time travel a few years now. He hadn't believed at first, but Eoin and Meehall had been able to predict too many things which came to pass. Ciaran had no doubt he would find himself in the future any moment now.

What was the future like? He had never asked Meehall or Eoin. Truth to tell, he had never dared to hope he would venture there.

Eoin stopped the wagon and closed his eyes, frowning in deep concentration while he clenched something inside his jerkin.

Nothing happened.

"Is it broken? Is it tae much that I ride along? Should we na hae tried tae bring the whole wagon?"

"Quiet," Eoin growled without opening his eyes or ceasing to frown. "Working, it is, but be quiet, or mayhap ye wull find yerself inside a wall in the future."

Chastised, Ciaran closed his mouth, fighting the doubt that crept into his mind. Was it a grand hoax?

No. The world started spinning around him, trees turning into a blur past his face. It was like the grandest dirt devil in all creation, and it made him thirst for whiskey. But it stopped just as suddenly as it had started.

It was nighttime here in the future, a strangely misty night with no clouds, yet hardly any stars. Ciaran wheeled about, making his kilt fly up as he peered at the sky. Where had all the stars gone? He couldn't dwell on that long, though, because the wagon had brought him into a castle compound larger than any he had ever imagined. A full dozen castles loomed around him, greystone edifices amid greystone streets, making him fall into battle stance and squint into the darkness, looking for threats.

Eoin jumped out of the wagon and beckoned for Ciaran to follow him through the huge door of one of these castles. It led into darkness.

Gulping down his fear, Ciaran did follow.

Now that he could see better in the dark, Ciaran doubted this was a castle. There was no finery on display in the hall. A monastery, perhaps?

They went down the greystone hallway, farther and farther into the darkness.

Wait. A light burned up ahead. An eerily steady light that didn't flicker. It was coming out of that doorway. Was someone awake?

THE KILTED HIGHLANDER CIARAN WAS ALL Nadia had been thinking about these past few days. How his mischievous green eyes sparkled under his long black hair. How his sword had rescued her from druid sacrifice. How impossible it was for her to be interested in him because he lived in 1706 and she lived in the 21st century.

With the idea of forgetting all about Ciaran, she had thrown herself into writing this historical article. Well, and for a chance at being accepted by the druids who ran Celtic University's historical society. And now, when she was in the midst of giving them her all, who should show up in the middle of the night when she was all alone in their office?

It would have been fine if it was just Ciaran. Him, she wanted very much to handle.

But Sarah's former friend John was with Ciaran, and she had told Nadia horrible tales about the man. He had deceived the Picts of old and almost caused the Gaels to wipe them out completely. Now, to be fair, John was one of the MacGregors who'd been cursed by the druids generations ago. He couldn't help but serve the druids.

Unlike Nadia, who was trying to please the druids for career advancement. Financial gain. Greed.

A twinge of guilt made her shiver as she stared at Ciaran and John. They had time traveled. The druids could do other things, but time travel was how they got all the cool or magical historical artifacts they wanted. And rather than spend time in another century aging and then return here to raise suspicion around what was supposed to be a respectable university, the druids had other people do their time traveling for them.

John was one of their lifelong servants, but she found it impossible to feel sorry for him.

Even as Ciaran spotted Nadia and smiled at her in joy at their reunion, John was nagging, "Come along now, Ciaran. We have a job to do, and while I know Baltair is as good as his word, I dinna ken how long he'll be able to keep the farmer and his family from investigating the woods. If they go and find the apple wagon has disappeared, they're likely to go get others to investigate. I ken I told Baltair he would be working for them a day, but I tell ye true: we have two hours at most before Baltair loses control of the situation..."

But Ciaran hadn't heard a word. His mischievous smile now covered half his face, and his green eyes sparkled at Nadia with all the trouble he thought they might get into. His long black hair was slicked back against his face. He was the most devilishly handsome man she had ever met and nigh the most handsome man she'd ever seen, in person or otherwise.

And she had his full attention.

He sidled up next to her, almost touching, but not quite. "What are you doing up so late?" He asked this as if he really wanted to know, as if he was curious about her life and genuinely interested in what she was up to. There wasn't a trace of suspicion nor anger nor annoyance. Not on Ciaran's part.

But John? That was another story. His nagging turned stern. "We dinna need to ken what she's doing here. We need to be on our way."

Flattered by Ciaran's attention, Nadia smiled back at him with her own mischievous smile. She wasn't quite promising to get in trouble with him, but she was suggesting she wasn't opposed to the idea. "I'm doing the same thing John —Eoin— is doing, trying to please the druids. Only I'm doing it on this computer."

Ciaran's gaze dropped from her eyes for what he plainly thought would be just a moment.

But Nadia saw the exact instant when he real- ized what an alien object sat there in front of her. She felt insulted for a moment. She was fully into the gaze they had been sharing. But then she imagined the computer as he saw it, glowing with light and seemingly reaching at her with its alien appendages. No wonder it distracted him. And he had been nothing but gallant with her misunderstandings of his time in history. Finding some patience, she again looked into his face.

Horror and wonder battled there comically. "Com pu ter?" he said the way a toddler would.

"Aye," she told him, unable to resist mimicking his accent. "I would tell you everything this computer can do, but it would take our whole lives and not finish the telling. Suffice it to say this is how I please the druids. While Eoin fetches things for them, I write stories for them. Stories that make this institution seem like all the others of higher learning in the modern world. I assume he's told you all about what they really do here, and that you appreciate what an important task I have." She sat up straight, pushed her chest out, and raised her chin up in the best imitation of someone proud.

It backfired a bit.

Ciaran's eyes went directly to her chest and lingered there longer than they needed to. He checked himself, however, and then a bit of fear took over his face. "Nadia, you shouldn't be alone where anyone can get to you. Have you a room where you can bar the door?"

This was an odd turn of topic, but she liked Ciaran, and so she answered him directly. "Aye, I have a lock on my door." She waited patiently for him to get to the point as she scanned her screen, reading the druids' request for an article one more time so she knew the details of what they wanted.

But Ciaran took her by the upper arm and tried to get her to stand. "That druid child Tahra and the Cameron clan could be anywhere, you ken. She didn't know the secrets of time travel a few days ago, but any moment now she might discover it and come after you. Allow me to escort you to your room and see you safely inside with the door locked. I ken you canna stay there always, but in the middle of the night like this when no one else is about, you should."

But she put a hand on his and gently resisted. "I will na. Much as I wish to go with you, I must do this assignment. 'Twould be different if you were going to stay a while. Perhaps you can help me with my assignment?"

Ciaran's smile broke out big again. "Aye. Aye, that I will. And should the need arise, I will do my best to protect you from the Camerons. Or Tahra."

She smiled at Ciaran.

He smiled back.

A deeper camaraderie bloomed between them, and she liked it very much.

Then Eoin had to go and ruin it. "Nay," growled the larger Highlander as he grabbed his distant cousin by the other arm and pulled him to the door. "I telt ye already, we need to get moving and return to 1706 before the farmer discovers we are gone. Are you daft, man?"

Ciaran struggled, but Eoin was far stronger, the type of man who is always lifting weights, even while sitting at table for dinner. Ciaran didn't even get a chance to say goodbye before the two of them were out the door and around the corner.

Taking casual notice of the thick leather gloves he wore, Ciaran struggled to get out of Eoin's grasp as his cousin dragged him down the cold greystone corridor of the druids' stronghold. The vastness of it made him fear for Nadia. Such power and wealth seldom treated its servants well.

"You didna have to do that," he told his cousin. "You could have given me a few moments with the lass. Certies even you could see she was pining after me the way I pine for her." English sounded so odd coming out of his mouth. To him, he was speaking Gaelic. The same magic that had brought him to the future was translating his speech.

The larger man held Ciaran fast. "I didna have

to bring ye along, and I have half a mind to return you straight away to our time and let you help Baltair keep the farmer and his family away from the wood. Ainly I ken your hearts wouldna be in it. Nay like the way Baltair's is while he is protecting ye."

Ciaran quit struggling. "What if I just shout out now, eh? Wake up the druids and bring them doon upon us?"

Eoin laughed. "I am their servant. Usually, that's a burden, but in this case? 'Tis you they would find fault with, especially and I dinna vouch for you. Nay, you will help me do what I came to do, and then we will leave this time."

Ciaran let those words reverberate through his mind while he slowly quit resisting and allowed Eoin to lead him through the greystone hallways lined with dark arrow-slit windows. As his resistance lessened, his wonder increased. "There are na flames inside the lamps."

Eoin answered with arrogant stoicism, not even turning to face Ciaran as he entered a corner tower and turned to go up three flights of greystone stairs. "Lamps here burn with electricity, the same force as lightning, ainly harvested and mostly harmless."

Ciaran wanted more details but could tell they would not be forthcoming, so he contented himself with gawking at the elaborate large lamp on the ceiling of the stairway tower.

When Eoin spoke again, his tone was hushed. "We're close to what I'm after. It would be better if you were quiet from now on."

They had reached the top of the tower, and Ciaran put his hand on the doorknob, only to find it locked. "How—"

Grinning like a seven-year-old, Eoin produced a key out of his sporran and fitted it into the lock, opening it with a click. Putting his gloved finger over his lips and signaling Ciaran to stand back in the shadows, he opened the door slowly, peering out into the dark room beyond.

When it was Ciaran's turn to go through the small door at the top of the tower, he gasped. It was dark, but there was a free flow to the air that let him know the room was vast. And it was full of shelves. On the shelves were all manner of things, but he couldn't quite make them out. His eyes hadn't yet adjusted to the darkness.

Eoin grabbed Ciaran's wrist and pulled him down one aisle and then another, plainly knowing exactly what he was looking for and where he would find it.

Ciaran's eyes were adjusting, but that didn't

really help him. There seemed to be no rhyme or reason, no organization to the way things were stored in here. Weapons shared shelves with jewelry, dishes, and musical instruments.

A ring caught Ciaran's eye, and he reached for it.

Eoin snatched Ciaran away before he could touch it, shaking his head at him with fire in his eyes.

Ciaran raised his other hand up in surrender, but he shot Eoin a look that said there would be questions later.

At long last, Eoin stopped and pulled an old halberd up off a shelf where it lay next to a gardening spade and a shepherd's crook. The halberd was undecorated and plain.

Ciaran raised his eyebrows at his cousin as if to say really? This is what we went to all this trouble for?

But Eoin just tugged Ciaran by the wrist back toward the door, which he closed and locked. Back down the spiral staircase of the tower. Back down the gray hallway past the room where Nadia had been toward the narrow greystone street where they had left the wagon.

When they passed the door, Ciaran couldn't help but notice no light came from under it. She must have finally taken his advice and gone to bed, fie upon it all. He should have a chance to talk to her. "I will stay here and protect Nadia," he told his cousin. "That druid child, Tahra, may be after her. You and Baltair can make do without me awhile. I ken you will be back here before long, aye? Take me back with you then."

Eoin tsked, took ahold of Ciaran's wrist again, and tugged him to the wagon. "You will do no such thing. What would Baltair and I tell Searc? We wouldna be able to explain your absence. Nay, you are coming with me."

They had reached the wagon, and Eoin pushed Ciaran up onto the seat before putting the halberd on the floorboards and then climbing up, himself.

NADIA HAD TO GET UP AND MOVE AROUND. SHE'D been sitting at this computer desk for hours, and that wasn't healthy.

She moved out into the hallway, and then, to the music that played through her earbuds, she danced the routine they were working on right now in dance class. She really liked it. Full of sways and long reaches, it did a lot to fill her imagination. The music was good too, a great modern Celtic ballad.

While she worked out the tension that had built up in the backs of her thighs from sitting so long, she kept an eye out. The far door down the hall had clicked shut when she entered the hallway. That door went up the corner tower to what she'd always thought of as a dead-end, because the door up there was locked. Apparently, the druids gave some people keys, because the guys had been gone at least twenty minutes and there was no other way out of the building. Eoin and Ciaran would have to come back through this hallway on their way out.

The music reached its crescendo, and she had to breathe deliberately in order to have enough air to do this part of the dance. Normally, she would sing through it and stretch her lungs as well, but something made her not sing this time.

If she was honest, that something was Eoin. The man disapproved of just about everything, and she didn't need his negativity when it came to her singing. Her deepest self came out in her song, more so even than when she danced. There was no way she was going to subject the true inner core of herself to Eoin's negativity.

Maybe there was time to get Ellie here with her before Eoin came back through. She stopped the song and texted her friend. "Eoin and Ciaran are here in the history building, upstairs for now. Back down any minute. Get over here."

She would have texted Sarah too, but just a few days ago, Sarah had moved to 1706 to be with Meehall. Nadia and Ellie were now the only two Americans in the secretarial pool at Celtic University.

It was stuffy in here. She needed to get some air. Out of habit, she turned off the lights as she exited the front door of the building, then looked outside and saw the apple wagon.

It looked both out of place and like it belonged here. It was from a different time, but it matched the architecture and the ancient feel of Celtic. She walked all around it, taking in the crates full of apples, the raised seat and running board where the driver would sit, and the pair of horses hitched up to it, patiently waiting with their tails swishing prettily.

"Couple o' kilted highlanders arrived in it, saying they had just bought it from a farmer," said a familiar voice she couldn't match with a name or face, an older man who belonged here on campus, but who for the life of her she couldn't place into a position, faculty or staff, student or parent.

She didn't really care, either. The only two kilted warriors nearby were Eoin and Ciaran. Now all she had to do was get rid of the old man so she could sneak into the wagon and go with them.

She turned to him, and when she saw him, he looked just like she expected him to. But she still had no idea who he was. No matter. She gave him a concerned look. "Really? They were just inside the history building a little while ago. They went upstairs and never came back down. I hope they don't disturb anything."

The old man's eyes turned a wee bit angry as he contemplated the history building. "Ye dinna say." He made his way up to the front door. He had to exert himself slightly to get it open, but open it he did. When he went inside, he didn't turn the light on.

Nadia didn't care why. She made her move. Looking all around to make sure no one could see her, she climbed into the back of Ciaran and Eoin's apple wagon and hid under a plaid blanket between two of the crates. The plaid didn't match either of their kilts, and it was lodged down so far between the crates, she doubted they were even aware of it.

Her phone vibrated.

There was a text from Ellie. "Are they still there? I'm in bed, but I can get dressed and head over!"

"No! I'm hidden in the back of their wagon,"

Nadia texted back to Ellie as fast as her thumbs would fly. "They'll be here any minute. I don't want Eoin knowing I'm here. I don't know how you would get in the wagon with me without him seeing you. Sorry."

"Whoa. I won't ruin it for you. Send Baltair back for me, okay?"

Nadia had to stifle a laugh, and she sent Ellie ten different laughing emojis before she texted, "Okay."

"I'm so jealous," Ellie texted. "This time, you're with people who'll know what's going on when you get there!"

"I'm so sorry. I wish you were here."

"Me too. You have to let Eoin know you're there, you know."

"I know, but I want to have something historical to write about first."

"Ha! You mean you want to wait and see if you can get Ciaran alone first."

Nadia sent Ellie an innocent angel emoji.

Ellie sent back a finger pointing at Nadia.

"I hear them coming!" Nadia texted as fast as she could. "Take care."

"You too. Bye."

"Bye."

The wagon lurched twice as the two beefy warriors got aboard.

Ciaran was beseeching Eoin. "You have the right of it. I dinna ken what you could tell Searc. But Nadia's in danger. I couldna bear it if anything were to happen to her."

Nadia's heart softened toward Ciaran even more, and she just had to peek up at the driver's seat from under her plaid blanket to see her protector.

Eoin put an arm over Ciaran's shoulder and patted his back, more in a way that kept Ciaran in the seat than made him feel reassured. "Look aboot you. This is a fortress. One druid child isna going to march in here uncontested. Although you mayhap should have told the lass to stay on campus and not wander off into toon."

Before the horses even took one step, the world was spinning around the wagon as if it were the agitator in an old top-loading washing machine, causing nausea, dizziness, and elation.

Nadia remembered this feeling well. It meant they were traveling through time.

S teady daylight, instead of darkness, indicated they had arrived in 1706. The world had stopped spinning, and Nadia's dizziness was subsiding.

But the horses had begun to step, and now her body was being jostled about much more than she was accustomed to in modern-day cars. She smiled. It was less bouncy than when she'd ridden a horse during her last time-travel adventure. This would do. She could even take notes on her phone while she eavesdropped on what was sure to be a juicy historic conversation. Thumbs poised above her phone, she waited under her plaid blanket in glorious anticipation.

"Why did we go tae all this trouble just tae get

that halberd?" Ciaran asked in a tone every bit as grumpy as Eoin's.

Ciaran's voice exuded the resentment he felt toward his cousin for not allowing him to stay and take care of her. This made Nadia smile some more. She wished she could jump out of hiding now and reveal herself, but if Eoin felt comfortable time traveling in this location, then she needed to wait until she was far away from it before taking the risk that he would take her right back where she came from as soon as he saw her. Eoin was a no-nonsense sort of man, and while Nadia normally admired that, in this instance it would not be convenient.

"'Twas what the druids sent me tae get," Eoin told Ciaran in a dismissive tone.

Ciaran was not to be discouraged. "'Twas locked up because 'tis a druidic artifact, I well ken. What does it dae? Why dae ye want it sae?"

Who cared? They needed to move on and discuss more historically notable topics. Still, she was growing bored, and she situated herself so that she could peek out from under her blanket.

Eoin didn't answer any more questions about the halberd. They didn't talk much at all as they went down a hill into a valley full of short trees, and then the wagon came to a stop.

Baltair's joyful voice preceded his bounce into the wagon by seconds. "Och, thank God in Heaven ye came back early! I didna ken how I would stand tae remain withoot ye!"

"Hold on! Hold on!" called out an older man from outside the wagon. "Ye promised me a full day o' this young man's labors in order tae complete the sale price o' my horses. If ye take him and them away now, then 'tis robbery, and I wull hae the constable after ye!"

Fear for the farmer flowed through Nadia's veins. The man was courting danger. Couldn't he see Eoin was dangerous? Wasn't he afraid?

But far from the grumpy tone he had used with Ciaran, Eoin's voice now came out silky smooth. "Here ye are." There was the clink of coins. "Does that settle us even?"

The coins clinked around a bit. "I suppose. Howsoever, if ye plan on taking the wagon back and forth across my land on the way tae yer camp, then ye wull owe me for the inconvenience. Those two are half my herd o' horses, and the others will whinny at 'em."

More coins clinked.

The older man's voice faded into the distance. "Verra wull. Ye nae hae the team and clearance tae traverse my fields. Dinna claim I ne'r did give ye naught."

Baltair socked Eoin's arm. "Ye are an auld softy, is what ye are. Dinna fash. Yer secret is safe with us. Aye, Ciaran?"

"Aye." Ciaran punctuated his affirmation by socking Eoin's other arm. "Say, think ye we ought tae get Searc's leave afore we—"

With the hand that wasn't driving the horses, Eoin grabbed Ciaran around the shoulders again, gripping him tightly while at the same time bursting into song at the top of his voice.

As I was a goin' ower the far famed Kerry Mountains,
I met with captain Farrell, and his money he was
counin'.
I foremaist produced my pistol, and I then produced
my rapier
saying 'Stand and deliver,' for he were a bold
deceiver.
Mush a ring um a dor uma da
Whack for the daddy-o.
There's whiskey in the jar.
I counted out his money, and it made a pretty
penny.
I put it in me pocket, and I took it home tae Jenny.

she sighed and she swore that she never would
deceive me,
but the devil take the lasses, for they never can
be easy.

This song was Irish and not Scottish, but she assumed Eoin knew that. It was her favorite from this time period, and she had to bite her lips to keep herself from singing along as he continued in his rich baritone voice.

I went up tae my chamber, all for tae take a
slumber.
I dreamt o' gold and jewels, and for sure 'twas nay
wonder,
but jenny drew me charges, and she filled them up
with water
then sent for Captain Farrell tae be ready for the
slaughter.
Mush a ring um a dor uma da
Whack for the daddy-o.
There's whiskey in the jar.
'Twas early in the morning, just afore I rose tae
travel.
Up comes a band o' footmen and likewise Captain
Farrell.

I foremaist produced me pistol, for she stole away me rapier.
I couldna shoot the water, sae a prisoner I was taken.
Mush a ring um a dor uma da
Whack for the daddy-o.
There's whiskey in the jar.
Nae there's some who take delight in the carriages a-rollin',
and others take delight in the hurling and the bowling,
but I take delight in the juice o' the barley
and courting pretty fair maids in the morning bright and early.
Mush a ring um a dor uma da
Whack for the daddy-o.
There's whiskey in the jar.
https://www.youtube.com/watch?v=V74Zucn9VSI
(YouTube: Whiskey In The Jar (Live) - Darby O'Gill)

Ciaran piped up with another ballad in his pleasing tenor, and the three men sang together, first that song, then another, then another as the cloudy Scottish sky drizzled on them and the wagon rumbled to rival the thunder.

All the while, Nadia was fairly bursting to join

in. Not yet, she kept telling herself. Wait until it will be too much trouble to take you back.

They were taking a break to drink some ale and catch their breath when Ciaran broached the subject of Searc again. From her last trip here, Nadia knew he was the Murray clan chieftain's war commander. Ciaran, Baltair, and Eoin were in his war party, which camped out here and there to be able to move at the ready. Just in case the Camerons attacked. Or the Murrays saw a good chance to attack the Camerons.

The Murrays were against a Scottish union with England. The Camerons, on the other hand? Their clan chief's son had been knighted by King Charles of England. They were not only Royalists, they were English Royalists. There was no love lost between the two clans.

Ciaran was asking Eoin, "Dinna we need Searc's approval for one o' us tae gae and join up at Cameron Castle? 'Tis a good idea, and getting this wagon sae we could make the trip there withoot being detected was far tae clever on yer part, Eoin, but willna Searc take issue with us doing someaught sae consequential on a whim?"

"I dinna ken sae," Baltair said brightly. "He has a respect for our cleverness, has Searc. There was that time we brokered the cattle deal, ye wull recall."

"Aye, that there was," Ciaran said to Baltair with an appreciative look.

Eoin flexed the muscles of his upper back in a show of strength that was every bit as impressive as it was intimidating. "And I were Searc, I would be quite happy tae hae the extra cattle, but ye hae the right of it, Ciaran. We dae need tae speak with him afore we press one of us intae the service o' Cameron Castle. For all we ken, he has some aught in mind, and we would scuttle it."

Nadia saw why Ciaran had brought this up. The path they were traveling —far too rustic to be called a road— came to a Y intersection here. On the left rose a pass through the grey-stoned highland mountains, while to the right lay a valley thick with heather, a good shallow place to cross the river.

Eoin hesitated a minute at the Y in deep thought before nodding with decision and turning toward the mountain pass. "Aye, we wull let Searc decide which of us wull be pressed intae servitude at Cameron Castle."

Nadia eyed the pass, calculating how far up Eoin would have to be before he wouldn't insist on turning back when she revealed her presence. Pretty far, she decided. Happy now for the plaid blanket, as the winds coming down from the pass were chill, she hunkered down between the apple crates, only keeping enough of the blanket parted so she could see what was going on.

The men sang some more to pass the time, and they were amusing in another way, too. Even though they were intimidated by Eoin —who in her opinion treated them unfairly— Ciaran and Baltair sidled up to their bigger cousin, taking every opportunity to punctuate what they said to him with small slaps, punches, and nudges.

Seeing they were an affectionate family in their macho way, Nadia didn't feel nearly so sorry for Eoin's wife as she once had. He was a good man, just a little gruff. In this period of history, that was probably a good thing.

They sang some more of her favorites, and she was having more fun than she had in months, probably ever since she started working at Celtic University. Sure, she took one ballads class and one dance class, but she couldn't afford to take more. She was there to work, and work she did.

Which reminded her. She was here to write an article to get closer to that promotion so she could afford the classes she wanted. Better note down what she had learned so far. The warriors of 1706 had war chiefs separate from the clan chief. The war chief took some warriors out and camped near the enemy's castle, waiting for the opportunity to attack. And of course men of this time had spies just like men of her time did.

She worried about Ciaran volunteering to go be a spy. It sounded dangerous. Worse, there was no way he would let her come along.

The road up the pass was steep, but the horses had no trouble pulling the wagon. It just was slow going. The singing helped, but she longed to be out there talking to Ciaran, not just watching him from under a blanket. And her muscles were getting cramped. Time to make her move.

But Nadia heard a different familiar voice from up the pass ahead. One she dreaded. "Who goes there?"

Ice ran through her veins, and she felt paralyzed with fear.

Eoin put on the reasonable tone he had used when paying for the horses. "Just some farmers taking apples tae market. We wull sell them tae ye, if ye want. 'Twill save us a trip."

The voice of Neas Cameron boomed out again from ahead. "Farmers? Since when dae farmers develop warrior bodies? Nay, we ken ye return tae the Murray war camp."

Along with Ellie, Nadia had been kidnapped by this man and his war party the last time she was here. She cowered between the crates, willing Eoin to whip the horses into a lather and mow Neas over. That was stupid, though. The Camerons were doubtless on horseback. What could Eoin do? She wouldn't complain if he took her back to the future this instant, but she knew he couldn't do that in front of hostile witnesses.

Eoin did whip the horses into action. They struggled and struggled to turn the wagon around quickly, but with the narrow path on the steep hill, it was hopeless.

Other voices echoed out in laughter. The Camerons had them trapped.

4

Ciaran could have drawn his own sword. It was right there in its scabbard by his hand, waiting to be drawn. He saw a man coming toward them quickly on horseback. Eoin had his hands full with trying to turn the horses to take the wagon down the hill, and Baltair was on the other side, sword in hand and ready to fend off attackers. But the halberd, the one Eoin had time-traveled to get, lay within reach on the floorboards, corralled from falling off by a hand's breadth of edging.

Yes, Eoin said the plain long staff topped by an axe the size of his head was for his druid masters and not for the three of them to use. Eoin spoke of nothing more than he did his druid masters, and this didn't surprise Ciaran.

It brought back the memory of the day Ciaran first met his cousin Eoin. Ciaran and Baltair had been at the deathbed of Ciaran's father and Baltair's uncle, Angus. The two of them hovered there, reciting the Latin prayer a priest had taught them. They didn't understand the words, but they were sure it was the right thing to do.

THE DOOR TO THE INN ROOM THEY HAD RENTED for Da's last day burst open, and Dougal Murray came in with a stranger. "Begging yer pardon, Angus, but this man has just shown up, saying he's yer kin."

Ciaran and Baltair met eyes. How dare this man intrude on such a private family time?

But Father held up a feeble hand. "I thank ye, Dougal. Ye did right tae bring him tae me. Leave us. We hae family matters tae discuss."

Da waited until Dougal had left the room at the inn and closed the door, leaving the four of them leaving the three of them alone with the stranger. "I can see that ye are a MacGregor. Ye hae the look o' my uncle, and also o' my grand da. From which time hae ye come?"

Ciaran met Baltair's eyes again. With their eyes the two of them said to each other:

"Och, nay, nay. Da has gone daft. Now we hae tae deal with the stranger on top o' watching him die. How dae ye want tae gae aboot it?"

"Ye gae right side and I wull gae left, and together we wull manhandle him oot the door. Ready?"

Meanwhile, the stranger played along with Da's craziness. "My given name is John MacGregor, but I gae by Eoin, John being sae English. I come from the twenty-first century. My father is Peadar Mac Dall—"

Father brightened a bit. He even tried to sit up in his bed. "I ken who Dall is. The tale o' his move from Kilchurn Castle under the Campbells intae the future under the druids has lived doon through the centuries. And likewise the tale o' his son Peadar's move tae the future from servitude in the new world. Ye come from an illustrious branch o' oor clan. More-over, we can trace oor ancestry directly back tae Dall, through his son Dombnall."

This got Ciaran's attention. He'd heard many stories of his great great-great-grandfather Domhnall.

How he had to make his way in the world when his father left. How he had been an illustrious warrior, resisting the purge of the MacGregors by the Campbells as long as he was able. How he had married and sent his children into hiding with the Murrays, yet still fought the good fight his own self, ever hopeful of fending off the condemnation of the MacGregor clan.

How did this Eoin ken the tale? Was it possible he was kin? Ciaran and Baltair both asked each other this with their eyes as they looked back and forth from Da to the stranger.

At last, the stranger shared a nod with father and then turned to speak to Ciaran and Baltair. "Aye, I wull ken the story o' yer forefather Domhnall. My uncle was the terror o' the Rannoch Moor. They called him a cattle thief, but all along he was merely getting back what was rightfully oors. The Campbells used him in his youth as their muscle tae secure the Rannoch, and then in his older years, the verra same men who had fought by his side betrayed him. I ken the tale o' how his son, my cousin, Gregor MacGregor —named for the namesake o' oor clan, the Viking king himself —how this Gregor son o' Dombnall fulfilled his father's wish and journeyed with his wife Molly tae Murray territory and proclaimed himself and his children after him for all eternity members o' the Murray clan."

Ciaran and Baltair relaxed. Ciaran put a hand on Eoin's shoulder. "There is na way ye could know that withoot ye being kin, sae be welcome in oor camp."

Da weakly cleared his throat and patted his bed on both sides. "Come. Sit doon with me. Hold my hands and comfort me in my last moments. Whatever Eoin tells ye, believe him. I was gaun'ae tell ye myself, but I hae run oot o' time. Ye hae the need tae ken afore ye wed."

It was a tad much, suddenly having another relative and then Da saying Eoin would tell them things he had meant to. But Da was dying. There was no time to waste on pettiness. Ciaran did as he was told, urging Baltair by gesture and expression to do the same.

Father's hands were cold and clammy. His heart could be felt to beat, but only just. The wound he'd received in the recent battle with the Camerons was taking him. It seeped blood out of his shoulder even as they spoke, but if the closeness was causing Da pain, he didn't mention it, instead clinging to Ciaran's hand for all he was worth.

It saddened Ciaran, how little strength Da had left, and he caressed his father's hand and arm, letting the tears flow down his face as he gazed in Da's eyes. "I love ye, Da. Save a good place for me up there in Heaven. I dinna care how large my mansion is, just that it be near yer ain."

This made Da smile, and tears ran down his own face. "There be a curse on the MacGregors, son, nephew. Aye, a curse even greater than the obliteration o' oor clan name by the Campbells." He looked to their new cousin. "I hae na the breath tae tell it. Ye must dae sae. Make taste, while I am here tae affirm it tae my son and my nephew."

At first, Ciaran kept his eyes on Da as the stranger spoke, only half listening, instead choosing to give Da his entire attention.

But Eoin's tale proved oddly compelling.

"...sae the druid had oor MacGregor ancestor betwixt a rock and a hard place. He could na get away withoot bargaining. Being a gambler with nary a child in his family as yet, he saw nay reason tae refrain from settling his debt with the fate o' his descendants. I wull save the details for another day and ainly tell ye: the fourth born son o' everyone in oor family is pledged tae be a servant tae this druid's clan o' druids. They have us fetch things, and mostly this means we travel through time. As I said tae ye da earlier, I am from the 21st century. I was born there.

And my father's Peadar, who was born in the 16th century o' Dall, before Dall moved tae the 21st century."

Ciaran felt lost, and he just stared at the man.

Caught up in his own tale, Eoin laughed, looking faraway. "'Tis an odd tale. My da moved tae my grand da's time when they were the same age, sae my grandda is maire like an uncle, and my uncles are maire like cousins—"

Ciaran had had enough. "Can ye na see my father must die soon? Leave off this foolishness."

But Da squeezed Ciaran's hand one last time, and the last words Ciaran heard from his da were, "'Tis all true, son."

EOIN'S DRUID MASTERS HAD ORDERED HIM TO get the halberd, so in a roundabout way, it was part of the family curse, too.

But what if it could help? What magic must it possess? Could it get them free of the Camerons' ambush? If they possessed something that could give them any advantage at all, didn't they owe their clan the courtesy of using it?

Besides, his curiosity was killing him. He would

be relieved just to know what it could do, and then he wouldn't need to wonder anymore. He could go on with his life.

Ciaran seized the halberd and raised it up just in time to fend off a Cameron on horseback. Rather than cut at the would-be boarder, he used the huge-bladed axe as a poker, and pushed the horseman away.

But that wasn't all.

The man lay still on the ground. And so did the man's horse.

It was as if two of them were made of rock, they were so still. Were they dead? Ciaran leaned over in the wagon to see them better. No, they were twitching as if they were trying their hardest to get up, but some invisible force was holding them down.

Ciaran turned the halberd around in his hands, admiring its abilities. What more could it do?

Laying his hands on Ciaran and Baltair, Eoin uttered an unfamiliar word, "Brothok!"

Ciaran felt as if he had just hefted a huge stone and thrown it as far as he could. As if he had just run for an hour and only now stopped to catch his breath, Ciaran bent over forward and sagged into the wagon seat. He only looked up because Baltair shouted at him and grabbed his arm, pulling him out of the wagon, which had stopped.

"Get on!" Baltair was yelling.

Ciaran shook his head to clear it and assess what was going on. Someone had cut the horses loose from the wagon. Baltair was on one and Eoin on the other. Baltair wanted Ciaran to get on behind him.

But that wasn't what caught his eye. No, what had Ciaran's attention, what made him stutter, gasp, and take a double and triple takes, was that all the Cameron men and horses lay paralyzed on the ground. It was as if he had poked each one of them with the halberd as well. He looked at it again, full of awe. "It looks sae ordinary. Who would hae—"

"'Twill last a scant moment!" Eoin yelled. "And ye hae na maire strength tae spare, aye? We must away!" The horse he was on danced around with his own agitation, frothing to turn and run down the hill.

Baltair's tug on his arm became even more insistent, and Ciaran followed it, getting on horseback behind the man and settling in. Ciaran's sword hung to his right, so he held the halberd in his left, resting it against his kilt.

Eoin rode over and held out his hand.

But Ciaran wasn't going to give it up. Och, nay. This thing was amazing. He held it close. If Eoin tried to pull it away, then he would pull Ciaran right off the horse, and Ciaran had some ideas what he might do then. Oh, he wouldn't paralyze his cousin. Not in front of all these Camerons, he wouldn't. But he might paralyze Eoin's hand, just to give the man an idea what it felt like to be helpless. His bigger cousin could do with a taste of his own medicine. He stared Eoin down, defying him to try and take the magic weapon.

Sighing and glancing toward where the Camerons were beginning to recover, Eoin turned his horse and took off down the hill.

Baltair kicked their horse into action as well, and just in time.

Because the Cameron men were getting up. The wagon was between them and Ciaran, but he got the impression that, had they tarried only seconds longer, they would've been captive. Or worse.

While Baltair coaxed the horse into keeping up a dead run down the hill, Ciaran turned to reassure himself it would take the Camerons too long to go around the wagon to follow them.

Ciaran's breath caught in his throat.

Nadia was in the wagon!

She was peeking out from under a blanket between two of the apple crates. She must've been there the whole time. Why had she kept quiet? Why hadn't she told him she was there?

Her eyes met his. She looked so afraid and yet so hopeful, it made his heart hurt.

"Baltair! Turn this horse aroond! Dae it nae, this verra instant!"

Baltair kicked the horse into faster motion forward.

5

Nadia cowered under her blanket between the apple crates in the front of the wagon's bed, silently cheering Ciaran on. She knew he wouldn't use that amazing halberd against his cousin, but she almost wished he would when she realized he wasn't going to get free in time to save her. Not right now, he wasn't.

But he would rescue her. She let this hope keep her from despair while the Camerons cooed over all the fruit and admired the strong wagon itself, hitching two of their riding horses to it. She itched to scramble out of the wagon and run, but the pass was too narrow for her to get away without them seeing her.

Two men she knew from her last trip here a few

days ago climbed up onto the seat to ride. Now it was more important than ever she remain hidden. She would look for her chance, and then she would sneak away from them. Ciaran would be watching the trail for any signs of her once he was able to, so she would stay near it and watch for him as well. She just had to make sure no one saw her, for they would certainly recognize her.

The Cameron warriors each took a handful of apples, stuffing extras in their shirts and making appreciative noises as they bit into them and licked the juice off their fingers.

"Wagon up front," said their leader. "The rest o' us wull gae behind and watch, lest aught fall oot."

Great. Well, she would just have to watch for her chance. She knew she would get one. She had to.

After a few hours, the Camerons' destination became apparent to Nadia as she peeked out from under the blanket. They were headed toward a large masculine home, made of fir planks. Standing guard on an isthmus between two lochs, it looked like a huge modern lake cabin, all made of wood and boxy shaped.

But she wasn't mistaken about what it really was: a fortress. There weren't any balconies for looking out over the lochs at breakfast, like a cabin would have. There weren't even any windows in the outside walls. It was big enough for a few hundred warriors, if they slept in bunks.

She knew the party she was with didn't stay at this house. They were a roaming war party much like the one Eoin, Ciaran, and Baltair belonged to, but Cameron rather than Murray.

Now that she had arrived here, she revised her plan. Now, she was counting on being able to stay in this house without being recognized by anyone who stayed there. Until Ciaran came to get her.

The Cameron warriors drove the wagon into a stableyard surrounded by the house. Sentries outside the gate had seen them coming with food and alerted a well-dressed older woman who must be the cook, because she came out rubbing her hands together and salivating at the apples, shouting out orders for so-and-so to carry them in and space to be made in her larder.

The warriors all clapped each other on the back and made their way inside, leaving the wagon in the stableyard, which was surrounded on all sides by the house and well secured.

Boys came out of the house toward the wagon now, and Nadia was shaking, she was so afraid. How was she going to hide her face when they removed the apple crates from the wagon? How was she going to get into the house, and once she did, how would she escape molestation.? Her jeans and tank top were hardly considered proper for a woman in this time.

An older boy, not quite a man but certainly trying to be one, solved her problem for her. Before he picked up one of the rough-edged crates of apples, he took off his long blousy poet-style shirt, and rather than let it fall in the dirt, he tucked it inside the wagon for safekeeping. Making manly noises, he lifted a crate and carried it toward the kitchen.

Nadia looked toward Heaven. "Thank ye." Not wasting one second in using God's provision, she hastily crawled forward under the blanket, snatched the shirt, and pulled it on over her tank top. Inspiration struck, and as she got up in the wagon as if she'd crawled up here to get a better look at all that needed to be carried, she wrapped one edge of the blanket around her waist and tied it into the semblance of a long skirt. There. Her jeans were hidden. Feeling very pleased with herself for keeping her hair long and natural, she crawled out of the wagon, turned and grabbed an apple crate, and followed the shirt-less boy into the kitchen.

He went downstairs into the cellar, where it was

thankfully dark, so the boy hopefully wouldn't recognize his shirt. She found the stack he was making down there and added to it, then followed him upstairs, but veered left when he veered right to go out and get another load of apples.

Judging by their mannerisms and dress, the women in the kitchen were all Cameron clan members, so it wouldn't do to hang about there. But she took hope from the way they treated the boy who had carried in the apples. He clearly wasn't clan, but rather a captive servant they didn't know well. And he hadn't been beaten. He was well fed and wore shoes. If they had one of these, then they likely had more. She looked for the next room down the hall, praying it would contain servants.

Fortune smiled on her, because the next room she entered was empty of people altogether, and wonder of wonders, it was full of ropes hung with drying laundry. She didn't need to wonder why they hung it indoors here in drizzly Scotland.

As quickly as she could, Nadia felt the laundry around her, looking for something threadbare. The women who commanded the other women were all clan, but those who did the more menial tasks? They were likely strangers to everyone but each other, captives like that boy.

The mostly dry, but very old and tattered, dress with the matching linen shirt Nadia found did much to relieve her anxiety. It did not look well cared for in recent times, clearly a castaway that was now worn by the servants. Hopefully, the servants shared clothing, and no one would call her out for wearing this.

She had hung up the plaid blanket to look like it was drying with the rest of the laundry —and was on her way to give the boy his shirt back— when one of the Cameron women from the kitchen entered, clearly someone's wife, as she was six months pregnant.

"Why dae ye linger here?" The Cameron woman took Nadia by the elbow and tugged her down the hall to the next room, a larger one, where half a dozen young women were washing vats and vats of laundry. Come to think, it looked like spring outside, and sure enough, they were washing all the bedding that had been soiled all winter. Mounds and mounds and mounds of linen sheets, as well as the clothing of the few hundred people who lived here.

This was the perfect cover for Nadia while she bided her time and waited for Ciaran's inevitable rescue, so she smiled at everyone and said in what she hoped was the right tone, "Verra wull, how can I help?"

When Nadia spoke in this time, she opened her mouth to speak in her American English, but Gaelic of the period came out. The last time she'd been here in 1706, this had shocked her. It didn't this time.

The pregnant wife threw up her hands and shook her head as she left the room. "I canna keep up with the humor o' ye young lasses. Get tae it. I dinna care what ye say or if ye sing, just get the linens washed."

Nadia waited until the wife was truly gone, and then made a show of relaxing. "I thought she would na ever leave."

The other women smiled the slightest, biting their lips not to smile too much. One of them corrected her. "That is Eimhir (AEveer), Sir John's wife. His father is still the Cameron, only he lets Sir John have most o' the authority nae, seeing how he's been knighted and all."

Nadia didn't quite know what to do with the reverence she heard in their voices for this Sir John. Did that mean they weren't captives, but members of the Cameron clan themselves? She didn't think it was wise to pursue that line of questioning. She had the MacDrest name she could use if they asked her clan. That had been the name Eoin used back in the time of the druids, during the second century. He'd been Drest, and he'd been back to see that his son had had sons. So they could be a clan. That was her cover clan, but she'd rather not have to use it.

Still, the woman who had spoken seemed friendly, so Nadia moved in next to her and started lifting the linens along with her, to dip them in the vat of who-knew-what over and over, then wring them out, and then put them in the pile of clean wet laundry, mere feet away from the pile of dirty laundry.

After learning her new friend's name was Mairee, Nadia said to her, "She said we could sing. Shall I start?"

Mairee and the others shrugged noncommittally.

Taking this as an invitation, Nadia started her favorite complex round. If they didn't know it, they would catch on easily enough. She knew the tune was at least as old as this time.

Rose, Rose, Rose Red
Will I ever see thee wed?
I will marry at thy will, sire,
At thy will.

It worked. After three repetitions, the others joined in, and after ten repetitions, they were singing it in rounds. Nadia introduced some complexity by adding a different verse to the round.

Aw, poor bird
You are sad,
But when you sang in yonder wood
Your song was glad.
Aw, poor bird
Fly away,
And in the treetops you will sing
your song so gay.

Thrilled to have gotten everyone singing both those songs in rounds together, Nadia joyfully added the third song into the mix, using the rhythm to dunk the wash as it plainly had been designed for.

Hey, ho, nobody home.
Meat nor drink nor money have I none.
Still, I will be merry, merry!
Hey, ho, nobody home...
https://www.youtube.com/watch?v=hgirEF4yd1I
(YouTube: Ah Poor Bird/Hey Ho Nobody at Home/Rose Rose)

Mairee tapped Nadia on the wrist. "Wull ye help me hang this, then?"

Nadia smiled at her new friend. "Aye, I wull."

Fascinated, Nadia watched while Mairee bundled all the sheets into a huge ball the two of them carried, balancing it on their chests between them as they edged down the hall sideways. They were rounding the corner into the hanging room, as Mairee called it, when Nadia heard Tahra's voice out in the hall.

"Weeks o' melting and forming, all ruined in a MOMENT! Whate'er shall I dae with ye?"

Paralyzed in fear, Nadia trembled in the hanging room, grateful for the laundry that blocked her face from view.

Mairee wasn't doing any better.

In response to Tahra's tirade, there was only a grunt, along with the sound of a man being whipped. Half a dozen warriors passed by the open door before Nadia was able to tear herself out of her paralyzed stupor and duck down, on the pretense of putting their load of laundry on the floor —when really she was hiding her face so that Tahra wouldn't recognize her.

The druid child Tahra —from whom Ciaran and the Murrays had rescued Nadia and Ellie— walked right in front of the door clutching a leather-bound book, screaming, "Nae I hae tae start all ower, ye sorry excuse for a man!"

Nadia didn't see the man, but the whipping sounds continued. The party had passed by the door and were getting farther away, so Nadia started to relax and breathe easier, comforted in the fact that she hadn't been recognized, at least not for the moment.

But then there was a bloodcurdling scream from the man, followed by gasps from all the other warriors in the hallway.

One of them yelled out, "Ye hae kilt him."

"Nay matter," said Tahra coldly. "Ye, Barrfhionn, ye are nae my leas-cheannard. Dinna make the same mistake the first one did."

The danger had passed. The voices were far away now, likely past the kitchen.

But Nadia was still shaking. Doing her best to imitate Mairee, who was picking up sheets and tossing them over the ropes stretched all over this relatively empty room, she asked in a shaky voice, "Does Tahra live here?"

Aside from a flicker of curiosity at hearing Nadia say Tahra's name, Mairee ignored her and kept silent, trembling just as much as Nadia was.

❧ 6 ❧

When they got down to the bottom of the mountain, Baltair turned the horse Ciaran was on to the left, opposite the direction they'd come from and not toward Cameron castle, either. Was their plan to ride around the mountain and still go see Searc?

Och, nay!

"We must gae rescue Nadia!" Ciaran urged. "Who can ken what they wull dae tae her this time? Last time they were gaun'ae sacrifice her!"

Baltair had slowed their horse to a walk, but he hadn't gotten down to walk it without a rider the way one normally would after such a run. Because he didn't want Ciaran to take off after Nadia.

Eoin spoke. "We need more people. I keep telling

ye sae, and ye willna hear. The Camerons wull hae taken her tae their stronghold betwixt the lochs. The three o' us dinna stand a chance against a force sae large. Nay, not even with the halberd."

While Baltair urged their horse into a trot — again, so that Ciaran couldn't get off without injuring himself on the rocks, Ciaran did what he'd done a dozen times already, called back to their bigger cousin over his shoulder. "Ye canna ken that!"

"And by the way," Eoin said in an offhand manner that piqued Ciaran's interest the way yelling wouldn't have. This sounded like something new, finally.

Alas, it was.

"That halberd is accursed. Whosoever uses it wull hae much power against their enemies, but they wull suffer an early and painful death. I didna get it for us tae use. The druids told me tae remove it from Celtic University, bury it up here in the highlands, and na tell anyone where."

Fear seeped into Ciaran's heart. The words Eoin had said rang true.

But he was a Scot, tough as nails. "Verra wull then, cursed as I am already, use it I wull some maire. 'Tis oor best chance against that druid child, Tahra."

Baltair responded this time, with a hitch in his

voice. "Ye dinna ken yerself tae be already under the curse. It may be that if ye stop using the halberd nae, then ye willna suffer the early grave. I dinna want for ye tae give up yer life tae this accursed druid tool."

Ciaran answered Baltair loud enough for Eoin to hear. "I'm willing tae dae sae for the sake o' my clan, and for the woman I believe I might hae loved. If I gae tae her now, with the help o' this halberd, mayhap I can pass myself off as some aught I am na. Mayhap the Camerons wull take me in, and ye wull hae yer spy. Eoin, ye ken its ways. Help me tae use it thus."

"Halt, Baltair," Eoin said from behind them.

Baltair turned their horse to face their cousin.

Eoin beckoned them over, and once they were huddled so all were in contact with him, he closed his eyes and concentrated again with that look on his face, out here in the Highlands in view of God, nature, and no one else, where they would return again from their time travel.

The world spun, but the horses, well-trained draft horses both, stood patiently still.

When they appeared back in the alley where they had last been with the apple wagon, it was again the dead of night, and Ciaran mentally congratulated whoever's foresight that had been. But he was impatient. "Why are we here and nay at the Cameron stronghold?" he growled at his bigger cousin.

Eoin took it in stride, deftly getting off his horse, tying it to a post, and gesturing for Ciaran and Baltair to do the same with theirs while he stood waiting. "I dinna ken how tae make the halberd dae a thing aside from paralyze the enemy. Howsoever, the folks who run this place dae, and sae I hae come tae ask them."

Again, Ciaran felt fear try and overtake his mind. Magic was unnatural, and though it was convenient for time travel, it certainly did have its perils. "And ye think they wull dae whate'er ye ask o' them?"

Eoin started them walking toward one of the dozens of buildings in this huge stronghold. "Och, nay. There be but one o' them who wull dae any o' my bidding, but she and I gae way back." He took out a slab of black glass the size of his hand and ran his fingers over it, then tapped it repeatedly with both thumbs for a few moments before putting it back in his sporran.

Lowering his voice to barely a whisper because he didn't know if anyone was around who could hear them, Ciaran asked, "Didna Meehall say Kelsey couldna be trusted?"

Eoin looked straight ahead. "If he did, 'tis news tae me." He walked past that one building and over toward a grander one a ways through the massive grounds of the druid fortress.

Ciaran drank it all in with unbelieving eyes. "Dozens o' huge castles. They must house thousands o' people! If the druids hae taken everything ower, here in the future—"

Eoin elbowed Ciaran in the stomach. Hard. "Dinna think those thoughts, leave alone voice them. Not here, and not anywhere. Howsoever, I tell ye true: Celtic University doesna hold even one o' every hundred people nearby. There are many more people in the future than during yer time. That is all."

They went inside the grand castle and up the stairs, then down a long hallway. All the while, the lamps lit themselves as they walked. Extraordinary! But Eoin had spoken of electricity to Ciaran enough times before that he realized this must be artifice, rather than magic.

Eoin must have woken Kelsey with his little slab of black glass, because she opened the door as soon as they knocked and was quick to invite them all three in and then close it again, twisting a small device inside the doorknob after she did. "So nice to see you,

John. These must be your cousins. Baltair, Ciaran, I'm Kelsey, and 'tis pleased to meet you, I am." She turned to Eoin again. "To what do I owe the pleasure?"

Ciaran studied Kelsey's face while Eoin explained that Nadia had gone back to their time and been captured by the Camerons, and the three of them wanted Kelsey's help, both to contact Nadia in her sleep and to get the halberd to disguise itself and Ciaran.

Kelsey didn't seem one bit surprised, and though this could have been because she had studied how to make her face the mask of the stoic as might be required from a druid, he didn't think so.

After Eoin finished, she smiled at Ciaran and spoke. "Aye, I will help you contact Nadia tonight during all your dreams. It will help if you all sleep here. It will be safer. I insist. I'll see that you go back to your time soon after you speak to Nadia so that you have plenty of time to enact any plan we make. As for the halberd and disguising it to help you become a spy, Ciaran..."

She made a show of tapping her fingertips against each other in secession in front of her. "I do believe that inside your dream is the best place for me to instruct you on that, as well." She gestured to three couches right there in her sitting room. "Now if you all will lie down and go to sleep, we can begin." Smiling at them over her shoulder, she went into the other room and closed the door. There was a definite click as she sprung a device in that knob, as she had in the door to the main hallway.

Eoin got up and went over to her door and knocked on it. "Let's look in on Meehall and Sarah as well."

Kelsey's voice came from the other side of the door. It sounded like she was already lying down. "Sorry, but the two of them have requested I leave them be."

✣ 7 ✣

Mairee had calmed down a lot since the incident in the hanging room, but she still wasn't the carefree woman who had sang rounds with Nadia. None of them were. The rest of the afternoon washing was somber. No one had been willing to talk about anything at all, let alone sing.

Did Tahra live here? Was it only a matter of time before the druid child recognized Nadia and reclaimed her lost sacrifice?

Nadia's stomach was eating itself up with worry. Dare she reach into her purse under her skirts and get out the Snickers bar she kept for emergencies? No way would she be able to explain the wrapper. Maybe if she unwrapped it in her purse? She looked around at all the somber faces and decided that since she had the means to cheer them a little, she should.

"I have some aught tae share with ye all," Nadia said to them as she put down the wash she was dunking and dug the candy out of her bag, unwrapping it first and then splitting it up into eight pieces. "Hae ye tasted chocolate afore? And peanuts? Caramel?"

Wide eyed, they all shook their heads in the negative and thanked her profusely as she handed them their share, then closed their eyes in bliss when they tasted the confection.

Nadia ate hers last, and felt instant relief when that small bit of sugar hit the spot and un-soured her belly. Almost at the same time, the scent of roasting meat wafted down the hall from the kitchen, making her stomach growl.

"Time tae tidy up the washroom sae we can gae help serve the supper," said the oldest among them, Sorcha.

Nadia couldn't put her questions off any longer. She had to know. "Will we serve the supper in the great hall? And does Tahra take her meals there?"

Mairee put an arm around Nadia. "Och, nay. Fear ye na. The wives serve their husbands. We are na allowed in the great hall. We stay in the kitchen and fill the serving dishes."

Nadia relaxed against Mairee. "Thanks be tae God."

Mairee and the other women crossed themselves and nodded in the affirmative.

For good measure, Nadia did the same, even though she wasn't Catholic. This was a way to bond with her new coworkers, and Nadia did believe there was protection in Heaven, just not in the act of making the sign of the cross.

They all entered the kitchen in accord.

"The food smells wondrous!" Nadia exclaimed when they reached the kitchen and she saw the roast being taken off the fire, the vegetables being taken out of the stew pot, and the fresh bread and pies coming out of the ovens. Seeing a stack of plates resting on the kitchen table nearby, she took one and went over to slice herself some of the roast and dish out some of the vegetables, fully intending to eat at the kitchen table, of course.

Mairee's voice sounded a bit high-pitched from behind her. "Och nay, Nadia. We dinna dish up the food for the men. The wives serve their husbands oot there in the hall. We dish the food ontae the platters. Here, I wull get ye one."

Nadia felt her face turning red. So even though they ate in the kitchen, they had to wait until the important people were served. She couldn't help but giggle a little, and when Mairee got close, Nadia whispered to her, "Ah, I ken. We're at the bairns' table."

Mairee's face was puzzled and concerned when she held out a platter and gestured for Nadia to dish some meat onto it. In fact, she had second thoughts and pushed the platter into Nadia's hands, gesturing for Nadia to hold it still while she dished the meat into it.

All eight of the women who had been washing together were busy like this for half an hour or so before the wives finally stopped coming into the kitchen for more platters of food.

Mairee patted Nadia's back. "Now we can get oor own food and sit doon at table."

Nadia saw why, too. They got the leftovers. The gristly ends of the meat and the soggy bottoms of the vegetables. The heels of the bread. At least there was butter. And oh! The food was delicious, nonetheless. She didn't know how long it'd been since she had a homemade meal. The slop that she ate in the cafeteria at Celtic was mass-produced quickly, 'meant to feed the body, but not entertain the mind,' was the motto of the druids who ran the place. Nadia had two slices of apple pie.

When all eight of them who Nadia thought of as washerwomen had finished washing their own dishes and then everybody else's dishes, it was dark out. She estimated it was 7pm or so, it being early spring and high up in latitude.

She turned to Mairee as the two of them rested against the huge washtub in the kitchen. "Now what dae we dae, sit roond the fire and tell stories?" She asked hopefully.

Mairee looked at her incredulously. "Nay, now we gae tae oor cots and fall asleep as fast as we can, sae that we get enough sleep afore we hae tae get the stove ready for the breakfast bread."

Nadia groaned and pushed away from the washtub, staggering as she stood and realizing she was very tired.

Mairee gestured for Nadia to help her get some heavy blankets out of a large cabinet at the end of the room.

Nadia rushed over and did so. "These are the heaviest blankets that e'er I did see. Is na there a warming fire in oor room at night?"

Mairee studied Nadia as if she were an alien from another planet. Her look was not unkind, just extremely puzzled. Before she spoke, she stole a glance at where the other six women were still drying dishes and putting them away, apparently deciding they were engrossed enough in their task not to have noticed Nadia's odd question. "These are oor sleeping pads. Spread them oot sae we all are as close tae the fire as we can be. We wull get the blankets oot next."

Nadia couldn't help herself. Her mouth started working before her mind could stop it. At least she kept her voice to a whisper. "Ye mean we are sleeping in the kitchen?"

Mairee looked at her seriously and whispered back, "Yer expectations in life hae been verra high." She waited, perhaps for Nadia to admit she was noble born, who knew. When Nadia didn't say anything, Mairee nodded the slightest, taking silence as an admission. "Aye, we sleep here in the kitchen. And we get up as soon as the fire dies down, tae build it up again afore Cook comes doon tae start the bread."

Nadia took three of the blankets Mairee handed her and spread them out on top of sleeping mats. "And how soon after sunrise is that?"

Mairee shook her head, scoffing in disbelief. "Well afore sunrise, Nadia."

In shock, Nadia took off her dress and hung it over a chair so it wouldn't get too sweaty and rumpled while she slept, as did all the other women. And then they all knelt on their pads and prayers together before climbing under their blankets on their pads, closing their eyes, and falling into an exhausted sleep.

She dreamed she was in an underground castle with amazing Celtic ogham carved in the walls. Wow. The only thing that could make this better was if Ciaran were here. There he was! Good. She deserved a nice dream after the backbreaking day of work she'd done.

Vaguely aware that other people were present, wanting to talk to her —why were dreams so weird like that?— Nadia only had eyes for Ciaran. Eyes, arms, lips, and tongue. The way it can only be in dreams, she was instantly beside him, throwing caution to the wind. She grabbed him and started kissing him with all the passion she felt when she looked into that smug little grin of his.

He kissed her in return, of course, it being her dream and all. But he had a style she'd never experienced before, and that was surprising, in a dream. Rather than wrestle with her tongue, his tongue caressed her cheeks rhythmically, causing her whole body to respond with the same rhythm—

All of a sudden, Nadia was sitting in one throne and Ciaran was sitting in the other, no longer touching her the slightest. Both of them were again fully clothed, though Nadia was wearing the clothes she'd been wearing today, not the tank top and jeans she normally wore inside the warm buildings at Celtic University. What the heck was going on?

Oh well, she would just wish him into her arms again, and there he would be ... And there he would be. He should be there, right?

"Just tell her, Kelsey. It's cruel to put her through this frustration, not to mention a wee bit embarrassing."

Oh no. That was Eoin's voice. And Kelsey was here? Wait a second. Hadn't Sarah said Kelsey could...

Nadia looked up and focused on the other people, who had been trying to talk to her: Kelsey, Eoin, and Baltair. She looked at Ciaran for his reaction to all this, a little bit afraid to see what it would be. But she relaxed when she saw him grinning at her with his mischievous smile and then raising his eyebrows in a "how about we do that again?" invitation. She smiled back at him before turning to the others.

Kelsey cleared her throat. "Aye, I have brought all these people to your dreams at their request, so that we can form a plan to rescue you."

Ciaran spoke from right next to her. "I need to get into the fortress as a spy so that we can find out the Cameron plan of attack, and tell the Murrays. You can let me in, and then I can help you escape—"

"No," Nadia exclaimed at Ciaran. "It's too dangerous. You can't stay here! You won't be able to bring the halberd, you know."

Kelsey spoke up now. "Oh, but he will be able to bring the halberd, if he gets it to disguise itself as a shepherd's crook or a walking stick or a plain old cane used by the infirm."

Nadia brightened. "It can do that?"

Kelsey smiled the slightest, clearly enjoying this. "Aye, it can do that."

Ciaran got up from the throne, and instantly the halberd was in his hand, used as if it were a cane. As soon as he did this, the halberd actually changed into the likeness of a cane, just the right height for Ciaran to lean on as he walked.

Kelsey clapped once and then hugged her hands together below her chin. "See, that's how it's done.

The same way in real life as you just did in your dream. Believe that it will disguise itself, and it will."

Ciaran marveled at his new cane. "What about the other wonders it can do? Eoin spoke to it before it paralyzed everyone that time. Is that its only trick, or can it do more?"

Oddly for her, being a druid and him just being a druid's servant, Kelsey turned to Eoin and gave him a look as if to ask, "How much do you want me to tell him?"

Eoin gave Kelsey a look as if to say, "Tell him enough that he can save himself, but not enough so he doesn't need me."

Kelsey turned to Ciaran. "It works according to your need. If you're in a pickle—"

Ciaran gave her the oddest look.

Kelsey laughed and looked thoughtful. "If you're in dire straits, or up a creek without a paddle, or at the end of your rope, or in any sort of fine mess—"

Baltair interjected, "Or three sheets tae the wind?" and joined Eoin in a hearty laugh.

Ciaran mock scowled, put his left hand on his hip, and turned on them with the halberd raised.

Instantly, Kelsey held up her hand.

Ciaran froze.

Kelsey's face was ash white and full of absolute

fear. "Never, ever even joke about using the halberd on your friends."

Ciaran stood there waiting for her to go on.

Kelsey just stared at him with her ashen face. She was almost trembling.

Ciaran nodded the slightest. "Verra well. I will not ever use the halberd on friends, na even in jest."

Kelsey waited still a few more moments, staring at him as if to measure how much sincerity had been in his statement. Appearing to decide there was enough, she went on. "Whenever you find yourself in danger, call on the halberd to do the most obvious thing that occurs to you —unless that would harm any friends. Do you understand?"

He nodded once. "Aye, I understand."

Baltair tapped Eoin's upper arm with the back of his hand. "What about the c—"

Eoin threw his arm around Baltair and squeezed so hard, the smaller man couldn't continue speaking. He then addressed Kelsey. "Thanks for explaining it to Ciaran so he can use it in order to spy on the Camerons. I take it this is satisfactory to you, Nadia. That now you will help him get inside the stable? We can have him there at dawn."

Nadia met Ciaran's eyes. They promised her a good time later if she would help. They looked amused at their circumstances —and more than a little pleased with the new knowledge of how much power the halberd had. She almost agreed immediately, but then she remembered.

"I will," she said. But when they all looked to be going on to another subject, she held up her hand. "I will, but on one condition."

Ciaran looked at her with mischievous curiosity, telling her with his eyes that he was more than willing to meet any condition she might set.

Eoin wrinkled his brow and looked down on Nadia. "You dinna get any conditions. You stowed away on our wagon, and stowaways dinna negotiate terms."

Behind Eoin's back, Ciaran rolled his eyes.

Biting her lip to keep from grinning and cluing Eoin in on Ciaran's disrespect, Nadia addressed Kelsey. "My condition is that I be allowed to stay and spy with him. I've already established myself here as a washerwoman. I've made friends with the other washerwomen, even giving them some of my Snickers bar to seal the deal. There's a lot they will do for me that they wouldn't do for Ciaran. I can help."

The men all voiced varying degrees of objection.

Baltair worried she wasn't up to it. Eoin thought she'd get in the way.

Ciaran was just worried for her safety.

Kelsey looked at Ciaran. "She has a point."

He opened his mouth up to say something.

Kelsey waved her hand in the air and got him to stop. "The halberd will protect her, too, at your wish."

He stopped and considered for a moment, then turned a thoughtful face to Nadia. "Aye, you can stay and help. But only if you do as I say. That is my condition."

"Works for me," Nadia said to Kelsey while locking eyes with Ciaran, calling his bluff with her stare.

Eoin and Baltair didn't look any too happy, but all Eoin said was, "Verra well. We will have him at Cameron stable at dawn."

The next thing Nadia knew, she was waking up in the dark on her pad on the floor of the Cameron mansion, next to a barely burning, cold kitchen fire.

❧ 8 ❧

Finally feeling strong again after a braw night's sleep in a wonderful bed —not to mention a bonny dream of Nadia— Ciaran kept a careful eye on Kelsey while she unlocked one of the three dozen castles in 'Druidville' and took him downstairs into a huge dungeon full of clothing. Among rich gowns, clerical robes, bardic costumes, truly the clothing of every walk of life, the underground room held kilts of many different tartans, some of which he didn't recognize. She gestured for him to choose one while she held out her hand for the one he was wearing. She seemed so businesslike about all this. As if it was part of some grand scheme. He didn't doubt it was, but did Eoin know that? Did it matter?

He pointed to a brown and yellow tartan kilt. "Which region o' Scotland yields these dyes?"

She smiled at him conspiratorially. "None. It's pure modern theater." She still held out her hand as if she expected him to disrobe right in front of her.

He raised his eyebrows at her, then looked at the stairs up to where Baltair and Eoin waited.

Rolling her eyes, she took the hint and left, flipping a switch that cast bright lights on all the clothing behind her.

Recovering from the sudden profusion of light and scarcely believing the wealth of wool and velvet down here, Ciaran chose a new outfit for himself out of the tartan Kelsey had assured him was only found in modern times. He appreciated the chance to do this. A highlander's kilt distinguished him, and while the clans didn't have official tartans, the regions where they normally harvested dyes did tell much about where a man hailed from. The less they knew about him by looking at him, the better.

He chose an older outfit, weather worn and unremarkable. He kept his sporran though, unable to part with it because his father had made it for him. And of course he had the halberd, but he was practicing disguising it as a walking stick, and because of that he also practiced walking with a limp. It didn't help his unmemorable and unremarkable image, but at least it would explain why he had a walking stick.

There was a mirror in the room, a luxury item mounted on the wall over a dressing table. Having only heard of mirrors and never actually having seen one, he couldn't resist looking at himself in it, practicing all his usual smiles to see what they looked like in clear view and not just in his reflection in water.

He had to admit, his face was darn charming. And far too memorable. It was his long hair, he decided, water slicked against his face and tied as it was with a leather cord into a ponytail at the nape of his neck. He took it out of the ponytail and combed it with his fingers till it hung down against the sides of his face. There. He looked much more like all the other warriors he'd ever met. But when he turned to go, his hair swiveled around his face, causing it to tickle his nose, and he remembered why he always wore it in a ponytail. There was nothing for it.

Not trusting Kelsey with this task, he sought out his cousin. "Eoin, you have to cut my hair."

Looking giddy, Eoin took to the task with relish, especially when Kelsey showed him there was a pair of scissors in one of the dressing table's drawers, so he wouldn't have to use his dirk. When it was all done,

Ciaran's hair was short enough that it wasn't tickling his nose.

He stared at the mirror again, looking at his new haircut from all angles, pleased with it. He was still strikingly handsome, but with this new hair and these new clothes, from a distance he would look like an entirely different person. Good.

Without ceremony, Ciaran and his cousins returned to their horses and then to 1706, arriving with plenty of time to get to the Cameron fortress by dawn. On the craggy highland mountain that looked out over it, still within the shelter of the trees, Eoin reined his horse in. "This is where ye dismount and gae on yer own, Ciaran. We wull bide here for two days only, sae ye hae two days tae spy. Then get back here, else ye are on yer own tae return tae Murray camp."

"Aye, we wull be here within two days' time," Ciaran told Eoin as he surveyed the way down to the fortress in the darkness. "Nay a moment tae linger if I am tae hae a chance o' meeting Nadia at dawn withoot being seen."

Eoin chuckled. "Use the halberd."

Wondering just what he meant by that, Ciaran dashed through the open ground to the first bit of cover, a clump of boulders a little way down the hill.

There, he looked for the next bit of cover, and so on. He was halfway to the fortress in this manner when he realized there wasn't any cover for the last fifty yards. The fortress was very strategically placed with this in mind, its perch on the small piece of land between two lochs making it impossible to approach without being seen. Why hadn't he thought of this earlier?

Eoin's voice came to Ciaran in memory. "Use the halberd."

What did that mean?

As the first ray of dawn beamed down into the heather and reflected off the loch, Ciaran saw Nadia in the stableyard, looking for him. The mischievous part of him wished he could just appear there in the stableyard without any warning and startle her, and he chuckled, imagining her face when he did so.

Ciaran nearly fell down. Energy was draining from him, just like it had when Eoin uttered that word and the halberd made all the Camerons around the apple wagon fall down paralyzed. A lot of energy, so much that it scared him. Now he was in no condition to run to the next bit of cover, let alone fight if he got attacked.

Suddenly, Nadia was right in front of him.

And he was in the stableyard.

Ciaran did what he'd wished he could do, reached forward with his left hand and tickled Nadia's waist, startling her into jumping straight up in the air and twisting around with the funniest look on her face when she saw him.

He opened his mouth to speak, but she put a hand over it, grabbed his arm with her other hand, and dragged him into the stable, thinking, "Is he daft? He canna be seen by anyone, let alone heard."

A memory of the druid child Tahra killing a man flashed through Nadia's mind, bathing it in terror at what might happen if Ciaran were discovered here and remembered to be a Murray.

She stuffed this memory and the fear it caused down out of her conscious thoughts, which raced on. "And how did he get in? If he's gaun'ae dae under-handed things like this tae me, then I dinna want him here. The nerve o' the man... Who am I kidding? O' course I want him here. He looks gorgeous with his new haircut!"

Wanting to hear more but unable to resist telling her he would not be leaving, Ciaran deliberately thought to Nadia, "There's not a chance I wull leave ye here by yerself while I can hear yer thoughts like this. We wull dae this together."

The two of them stood in an empty stall in the

near dark of the stable, but he could see Nadia's eyes open big.

She didn't look afraid, more embarrassed. And intrigued. "How are ye doing this?" she asked him in her mind while at the same time testing his thoughts out, seeing how much she could discover!

He mock scolded her for her boldness with the color of the words he thought toward her. "Eoin suggested I use the halberd for things I dinna understand how tae dae, and 'tis working. It got me inside the stableyard from a hundred yards away, and now 'tis allowing me tae speak with ye withoot alerting the others."

Thoughts of the early death he was cursed to because of the halberd tried to surface in his mind, but he shoved them away, lest she hear them and despair. There was no help for him. He had already used the halberd. The curse was already on his shoulders. He was going to fully enjoy the short time he had left in the world, and that meant being in the company of a Nadia who wasn't terrified about his fate.

Nadia was still holding him by the arm, and the contact was at the same time both not enough and far too much. If he could be sure they wouldn't be interrupted it would be a different story, but...

As if Ciaran's thinking about it had caused it to happen, the door at the opposite end of the stable rattled and opened, letting in the light of the sun that had at last risen. The man who had opened the door spoke to the horses like a father. "Ye need a bit o' work there on yer left rear shoe, aye?" Down to the next stall. "Wull the flies are getting tae yer hindquarters, eh? We'll see if we canna get ye some ointment for that." Down another few stalls. "Och, such a pile ye hae made owernight! Were things sae easy ye had sae much time tae eat grass yesterday?"

Ciaran cast about for something to do to look productive in here so that he wouldn't be kicked out immediately.

Nadia thought at him, "Grab that rake and start mucking out stalls!" Her choice of words was odd, but the clear —and amused— vision she showed of him clearing the horse dung away from the straw left nothing to his imagination.

He cast about in his mind for some other way, any other way, to look useful, but came up with only impractical ideas. Grooming horses that had just slept the night. Going out to bring in feed when he had no idea where it was.

"Good idea," he told her even as he shook free of her and went out to grab the rake that leaned against the wall by their empty stall. He got to work immediately, not taking any time to say hello to the stable master or even acknowledge his presence. "If he first sees me working, I wull hae the best chance o' being allowed tae bide."

The flavor of Nadia's thoughts was troubling, and when she spoke to the stable master, she confirmed she was having fun at Ciaran's expense. "Top o' the morning tae ye, stable master. Bixby here came at the same time I did, but he has been hiding because he's lame, and a bit addlepated. He was afraid ye lot will cast him oot rather than give him something useful tae dae. He can dae work, see?"

Fuming, Ciaran had no choice but to pretend to be an incompetent man named Bixby, of all things. He did look rather silly holding the walking stick with one hand and the rake with the other, and he wasn't about to set his 'walking stick' aside.

Nadia was laughing furiously in her mind. This wouldn't do. Ciaran thought deliberately at her, "Aye, ye hae won the moment, but I shall win the day, mark my words."

In their heads and silently, she laughed all the more at his threat.

He really couldn't blame her, seeing the ridiculous position he was in. Darn it.

The stable master was looking thoughtful whenever Ciaran glanced his way —which was not often. Ciaran was giving the work his best effort, under the circumstances. His full attention, anyway.

"My name isna stable master. Call me Ruadh. And I will give ye a try, Bixby. Ye dinna merit sleeping anywhere but here in the stable, which I reckon ye hae already found tae yer liking, sae ye may abide. But more than raking dung, I want ye tae go along out in the fields and help the lads bring in the cattle for milking."

Outwardly, Ciaran tried his best to look slow of mind, yet grateful for the opportunity. "I thank ye, Ruadh." But inwardly he rejoiced with Nadia. "This is oor chance. We can gae up and report tae Eoin what we hae learnit sae far. And we can beg him tae bide another two days sae we can learn more." He played like he was falling. "Ye wull want tae help me, seeing as how I'm lame and all." With that last thought, he grabbed her and used her to lean on, tickling her ribs as he did.

She elbowed him in the side to disguise her laugh and his tickle and then elbowed him again for good measure as the two of them headed arm in arm toward the front gate. But all the while, she was thinking about the first time they met.

She'd been tied up on a stone slab in the sacred grove waiting to be sacrificed. She had seen him rushing in with the other Murray horsemen, her friend Sarah, and Eoin's brother Meehall. Ciaran felt in her mind how much she had admired his ability as a swordsman when he fought Tahra, before the druid child almost killed Sarah with her magic. But Sarah had freed Nadia and Ellie, and together they had lit the sacred grove on fire. Tahra had fled then, bereft of her magic, which came from the plants and taking the surviving Camerons with her, to fight another day.

He relented then and showed her the way he had seen her that day, not even a week ago. He showed her how beautiful she was, how graceful. He had resolved, the moment he saw her, that she should be loose and carefree and dancing out in the field under the moon at planting.

They held each other a bit tighter as they approached the front gate

"Hae ye e'er been marrit?" Nadia asked him in her mind. Her thought was curious, and prepared for grief. She was ready to console him if he was a widower.

With the color of his thoughts, he let her feel how grateful he was for her planned offer of solace.

Talking with her this way felt so intimate, more so than anything physical they could do. It made him a bit giddy. "Nay, hae ye?"

Her answer came to his mind sweetly, like a favorite memory. "Nay. Folk get marrit older in my time, na till they are five and twenty at the least, and more often na till they are thirty."

He could tell she was sincere, but with the flavor of his thought, he playfully called her on it. "Nay!"

Her thoughts tickled his mind. "Aye, I telt ye true! Sae why hae ye na been marrit, Ciaran? Dinna folk marry quite young nowadays?"

He tried to keep up the light mood, but her question brought him back down to the earth beneath his feet. Not sad, just serious, he caressed her mind with his to let her know he didn't resent her for changing the mood. "Aye, we dae marry young, but ever syne Baltair and I started running about with Eoin, the lasses hae shied away from us. Till ye and Ellie showed up and took an interest."

She pushed him away, playfully.

Holding the halberd sideways as if it was weak and unable to support him compared to her, he made a big show of limping so that she had to hold him up.

She tickled his mind with hers. "Wull, I would tell ye 'Sorry tae hear the lasses shunned ye, but ye would ken 'twas a fib. I always thought 'twould be convenient, the ability tae read thoughts, but now I am na sae certain."

He sent mental caresses. "Certies, ye jest. This is amazing. And I wouldna want tae share this with anyone more than with ye."

She relaxed a bit in his embrace, so that he was the one who reached out to open the gate. So close. They came so close to having a field day together.

An authoritative woman's voice called out, "Nadia! What dae ye oot here? Get in the house and make up the beds."

Desperately, he tried to hold her mind close to his. "Canna ye tell her ye hae other orders already?"

"Nay. Ainly the clan chieftain can gainsay her. 'Tis his wife."

Reluctantly, the two of them parted.

❧ 9 ❦

Nadia's attention was ripped away from Ciaran at the same time her mind was torn away from his by the distance between them. Just a foot did it. One moment, her consciousness was comfortably bathed in the warmth of his. The next moment, she was alone, and being sternly told what to do.

"Start yer straightening up in Tahra's suite," said Eimhir (AEveer), the chief's pregnant wife.

Unable to form words, the idea of going near Tahra horrified her so, Nadia just stood and blinked stupidly at the finely dressed woman.

Eimhir responded to Nadia's blank stare by adding, "Tahra's suite is above the stables there, dae ye see the windows?" When Nadia still didn't start moving, Eimhir threw up her chin and took Nadia by the hand, tugging her into the kitchen door after her. "Gae through the kitchen this way, through this door intae the main hall, and then up the stairway on the north wall..." She huffed up the stairs, tugging Nadia after.

At the top, there was a balcony that looked out over the great hall, with only one set of double doors which must go into Tahra's quarters. Sure enough.

"Through there, lass." Eimhir gently pushed Nadia toward the doors the way a parent sets a toddler to walking. "Dinna fash sae. Ye didna spoil her plans the way that lad did, sae ye hae naught tae fash aboot. See that ye get her rooms tidied up, and then gae across the great hall and up tae oor quarters and his parents'. When ye hae finished with that, gae doon intae the general quarters. Matilda has taken ill this day, and ye are the next most spry lass. See that ye earn yer supper." And with that, the knighted Cameron's wife huffed back down the stairs, leaving Nadia standing trembling in front of Tahra's door.

It wouldn't be too bad. She would keep her nose in her work and her face turned away from the druid child. She was wearing a very different outfit now than she had been then, and her hair was covered in a dust cap Mairee had found for her, so there was no reason Tahra should recognize her. Thus bolstering her confidence, Nadia knocked on one of Tahra's huge double doors.

The druid child's voice came from deep within her quarters. "I'm in the bath! If ye are a lass come tae dae the straightening, get tae it. If ye are a lad, then dinna enter."

That was a relief. If Tahra was in the bath, then she was much less likely to see Nadia. Much less likely. With that thought to buoy her spirits, she resolutely pushed the double doors open and entered the druid child's quarters.

Tahra lived like a queen. She had a king-size canopied bed on a raised platform in the center of the room. It had heavy drapes that could be pulled around it, and three goose-down comforters had been shoved to one side. Nadia started there, making up the bed and straightening the drapes. She could hear Tahra all the while, talking to her maids, who were assisting her in the bath.

They fawned over the druid child.

"Why hae we been here sae lang, mistress? Why dinna ye open one o' yer portals and take us somewhere else?"

"Aye, 'tis such a grand time when ye make a

gateway and take us through tae anoother place. The grandest time o' all."

"And how soon wull we gae intae the future as ye said?"

Nadia cringed with every impertinent question they asked, expecting to hear the whip any second.

Unlike when she spoke with her male warriors, Tahra's tone was indulgent now, with the maids. "'Tis different this time. That fire which forced us tae leave the sacred grove drained someaught from me that doesna normally drain. 'Twill take me longer tae regain my strength. Och, aye, that's the spot what itches most."

"'Twill take longer this time, but next time ye wull take us intae the future, aye?"

"Eventually I wull. Perhaps na next time."

"Hae not we been good enough? Are we not loyal enough? Dae ye na feel cared for enough?"

"Ye dae a fine job o' it. Dinna Fash. 'Tis not o' yer doing, this limitation. I hae not discovered the secret o' gang tae the future yet, nor tae the past. Soon, I wull. O' that, ye can be certain."

They all cooed at each other companionably to the sounds of the water swishing and dripping.

"So ye will na gae withoot us?"

"I didna say that. Nay, I must gae learn tae gae

through time. But if I canna take warriors, then I willna take ye. Nay, I must gae alone, betimes."

"Na now."

"Nay, na now."

The tones of their voices were so sickeningly sweet, Nadia wanted to turn around and leave the room immediately, but she saw an open book across the room. An important book, and treasured, by the binding and by the way it was mounted on a pedestal. Wait, it was the book Tahra had been carrying just before she whipped that man to death.

The book called to Nadia, but she dared not go straight to it, lest one of the maidservants come in and see her and ask questions. She had to work her way around the room.

While she dusted her way along a huge dressing table with a mirror and dozens of clay jars full of ancient cosmetics, she couldn't help recalling what it had felt like to share consciousness with Ciaran. Home, that's what sharing her mind with the smirking highlander had felt like. Being in her true home, not in her dorm room at Celtic University, but back in her grandmother's home in New Hampshire. There, every item was lovingly placed and every guest was lovingly welcomed.

Ciaran's mind was mischievous, yes, but not evil.

It was playful, like most young men's, but rather than video games or sports, he played in practical jokes. The times he lived in made his practical jokes much different from any she had heard of before. It had been such fun to glimpse his memories of them, especially the time he put Senna tea in the warriors' ale and warned no one but his cousins, who all laughed when everyone else ran for the bushes during the bonfire that evening—

The sound of someone standing up in the bathtub made Nadia feel faint. Taking deep breaths and grabbing hold of the dressing table and steadying herself so that she could make a dash for the door, she only barely heard what was said in the bathroom.

"Wull ye turn roond sae we can wash the back o' ye?"

"Dae ye want for us tae wash yer hair?"

"Aye," said Tahra, "the grove near here is dirty, ye ken."

Nadia relaxed against the dressing table when she heard Tahra get back into the bathtub, accompanied by the sounds of water being poured over her head.

Whew. She had a while. Heart pounding, Nadia crept straight over to the history book, dust rag in hand just in case anyone came in. If they did, she could appear to be dusting the book, rather than pouring over its contents. She gasped. It was a history book. From the future, 1918. Oh no. Tahra knew what was going to happen before it happened.

The history book was open to a page that said, near as Nadia could tell in a strange version of Gaelic:

...the Murray-Cameron battle raged on,
but when the Murrays won the day,
it secured their place in the mind o' the monarch...

Desperate to get any information she could about the specifics, Nadia skimmed down the page, looking for dates and names. She nearly fainted again when a name bounced out at her.

...One warrior in particular, Ciaran Murray,
was instrumental in the Murray victory...

Tahra knew Ciaran's name, and that he would be crucial in blocking the druid child's efforts to get the Camerons ahead.

Nadia rushed out of the room before she was discovered.

❧ 10 ❧

Ciaran couldn't help leaning on the 'walking stick' as he followed the three other men out into the fields to round up the milking cows. If anything, this use of its powers had weakened him even more. If last time was any indication, it would take him all day to get back enough strength to defend himself properly, let alone use the halberd again. Oh well. This weakness played into his disguise as a lame man and taught him the movements he needed to play the part convincingly. He was thankful that he got stronger and stronger, yet could maintain the façade of being lame.

In truth, the hardest part was remembering to

answer to the absurd name Nadia had given him, Bixby.

At first, the men all stayed together. Most of the cows had stayed together as they were wont to, especially those with calves, and the four kilted men easily got over to the other side of the herd and urged them on toward home.

The trouble was, Ciaran had to keep playing slow in the head while using the 'walking stick' to compensate for being lame. Which meant he had to move slowly.

And like cows everywhere who have been eating grass all day, these had a load to dump. And equally like cows everywhere, they all dumped as soon as they were made to move.

So 'Bixby's feet got much more soiled than Ciaran's ever had. This was all down to Nadia and her notion that he was addlepated! He would find a way to pay her back, oh yes he would. She didn't know who she was dealing with. Baltair had tried more than once to get the best of Ciaran, but Ciaran had always come out ahead. Until one day, Baltair had sworn off trying altogether. Ciaran still smiled, remembering how Baltair's face had looked when he realized he had not his own plaid belted about himself, but his mother's.

Two of the men took the easy cows home, along with all the calves, leaving Bixby and one other man to get the more stubborn cows down from the grassy patches up on the surrounding mountains.

"'Twill gae quicker if we split up," the other man told 'Bixby'. "There are two unaccounted fer, but nay matter how many ye find, be back at the gate by sundoon. They willna open it after that."

Ciaran stumbled around till the man was out of sight and then, grateful for the chance to at last stretch his legs for real, climbed up his mountain in earnest. By now, he was well familiar with the Cameron branding mark on each cow's rump. It was easily visible from a distance, so long as the cow wasn't lying on her side, and so he had no doubt he could identify any cattle he found as either Cameron cattle or someone else's. The penalty for herding in someone else's cattle was steep, and he had been warned to take care not to do so. That the penalty would fall on him. Death.

Struck with the irony of that threat, he laughed to himself a wee bit. Little did they know he was marked for death anyhow. But with this thought came the memory of Nadia's mind caressing his own, and a deep sadness overtook him. Would that he could start a life with her, have children with her. He would even go to her time if she didn't want to stay in his, just to be with her.

He was so taken up in these thoughts —and so sure no one else would be up here on the mountain— that he didn't realize Dolaidh (DO nee) was there until the man was talking to him. Fortunately, Dolaidh didn't recognize Ciaran from the incident at the apple wagon, but Ciaran sure remembered Dolaidh. For that reason, he knew the man was usually with the war party, and it gave him a good retort to the man's greeting.

"Two o' them ower here! Come help me surround them."

"Yer a warrior, herding coos?" said 'Bixby,' careful to sound addlepated.

Dolaidh laughed good-naturedly. "Sae ye hae me figurit, eh? Aye, 'tis scouting I am. Dinna fash. Nay Murrays lurk within site o' this mountain. Thought I might as wull bring the coos doon with me. Why had ye na yet brought them? And ye are new. How are ye callit?"

"I am Bixby." Ciaran clumsily gestured to his walking staff and then pointed to his leg, which he made a show of not standing on. "Why hae ye na taken them doon already?"

Dolaidh led 'Bixby' around to the other side of

the cows so that the two of them could herd these stubbornest of the Cameron bovines down mountain. They were in position now, and out of habit, Ciaran locked eyes with the other man so he could nod when the two of them would rush the cattle.

Dolaidh raised his eyebrows in disbelief.

It took Ciaran a moment to figure out why, to remember that 'Bixby' was lame. He pursed his lips ironically to get the man's attention, and then he used the 'walking stick' to go as fast as he could the way they had come.

Dolaidh held up his hand to admit 'Bixby' was up to the task, and once again nodded when it was time to rush the cattle from the direction opposite where they wanted them to go.

They did, and it worked. The cattle ran down the mountain a ways to the next patch of grass.

Casually as they walked down there, Dolaidh told him, "Ye said sae yerself. I'm a warrior, na a coo herder. And I shall fight Murrays on the morrow, whilst ye stay here with the lasses." He slapped 'Bixby' on the back conspiratorially. "I dinna suppose ye hae it sae bad, eh?"

11

Nadia grew anxious as she scrubbed the stew pot in a wooden half-barrel tub of lukewarm water with a rock and a plaid woolen rag that had seen better days. It was nearly dark outside, and Ciaran hadn't come back yet. Was he all right?

The mood among all the women in the kitchen washing the supper dishes was somber as usual. They weren't allowed to sing in the kitchen, only downstairs in the washroom. Everyone was singing out in the great hall, but the song was a sad one for Nadia. It was a fighting song, and all the warriors were in high spirits. All their talk was of attacking the Murray clan.

Gently, Mairee eased her way in between Nadia and Sorcha to help scrub the pot. Mairee's presence comforted Nadia. She longed to ask after her new friend's family and her life so far, to get to know Mairee. But she didn't dare. Best to keep silent and wonder, rather than open one's mouth and be sure of opposition. Because difficult as it was to think of these new friends as potential enemies, Nadia knew beyond a shadow of a doubt that if they had any loyalty to the Camerons, they would hate the Murrays. And Nadia knew she would hate them in return, even though she liked them very much as individuals and had nothing against them, personally. Far from it.

With Mairee's help, the pot was getting clean much faster, and Nadia smiled at her friend whenever they met eyes, which was quite often, there being nothing else to do. They didn't dare speak even about mundane neutral things, lest they interrupt the revelry in the next room.

And then Nadia felt Ciaran's presence in her mind and was both relieved and more anxious. His feelings for her were tender and affectionate and welcoming, which felt wonderful. But the words he formed in their mingled minds alarmed her.

"They wull attack the Murrays tomorrow! We

need tae gae! Can ye get oot tae the stableyard in the night?"

In her mind, she rushed into his arms and hugged him tight. "Aye."

He returned their mental hug. "Dinna gae tae sleep yer own self."

She shifted to emotions rather than mental imagery, bathing his mind in her confidence at being able to take care of herself. "Dinna fash. I hae some aught I can take for wakefulness."

Surprising her, his mind shifted immediately to a panicked alarm that was so strong, it made her own heartbeat speed up so that Mairee noticed and looked around for the threat.

Nadia shook her head and gave Mairee an embarrassed smile, as if she's misheard something banal.

Meanwhile, Ciaran's mental panic continued. "Some aught the druids gave ye? Nadia, there are big dangers in trusting their magic, ye ken—"

She let him feel her gentle humor at that last line and waited for him to calm down before she answered him in her mind. "Nay, naught from them. Some aught harvested from beans, called caffeine. I hae it in tablets that ye swallow."

His panic receded in waves like the ocean tide,

but much quicker. "Verra wull, I suppose that is safe, then."

She tried tickling his mind with her humor, gently, to keep the mood light and help him save face. "Shall I bring ye one?"

Instantly, he was once again in protector mode, and it looked a thousand percent better on him than his worry had. "Nay. Nay, 'twould rouse their suspicion, ye ken?"

Wishing to maintain her air of self-confidence and independence, she splashed him with just a bit of her humor. "Aye. Verra wull, I wull wake ye."

He resisted, making his mind a strong tower of manly resolve. "I'll be waiting for ye. I hae tae gae now. 'Tis sorry I am, but I can ainly rake this strip o' the stableyard sae lang.

"I wonderit how ye were dang this. I understand. Anon."

Nadia managed to take two caffeine tablets when she went to relieve herself in the chamber pot they kept in a closet down the hall. She felt fine passing water there, but not the other, and everyone knew it. This had been a source of embarrassment, but now she was glad.

One last time, Nadia helped Mairee put the sleeping mats and blankets down, said her prayers along with everyone, and lay down on a pad on the kitchen floor. When all the other washerwomen were asleep, she slowly got up, dropped her blanket down in a rumpled mess on top of her pad, and nonchalantly walked to the kitchen door.

Sorcha looked up when Nadia pulled the latch.

Nadia did the potty dance.

Sorcha rolled her eyes and turned over on her pad, wriggling to make herself as comfortable as she could be on the floor.

Nadia went out into the moonlight and crept across the stableyard full of cows. Cringing each time one of them mooed, she made her way over to the stable's outside wall where Ciaran's empty stall was. There in the shadows of some barrels which protected her from the cows, she crouched down as if to do her business.

Mercifully, Ciaran's consciousness came into hers right away. She wouldn't need to wake him.

"Is the courtyard clear?" his mind asked hers.

"Aye, unless ye count the coos."

"Good. Bide there. I'm coming."

"But there are guards. How wull we get through the gate, leave aloone off the isthmus, withoot they ken it?

"I hae been listening. Ainly two guards hae the

night duty, and they cross one another at the gate on their rounds."

He was in front of her now, and her barrel enclosure was crowded with the two of them.

She looked up into his eyes with rapt interest in his plan, impressed with how sure he was of himself. "How will that help us?"

Ciaran took her hand. "When they're taegither by the back gate, come with me and ye wull see. I hope."

"Ye hope?" With their minds mingled like this, she could tell he was mostly joking. It was that small part of him that was a bit worried that she paid attention to, though, along with the mooing cows. Pleasantly, he found their wanderings easy to navigate, and while she was with him, she didn't fear having a foot stepped on.

When the two kilted Cameron guards were close to meeting by the back gate, Ciaran ran through the cows with her.

"What are we dang?" she asked him in her mind. "The idea is tae escape their notice, na tae—"

As soon as she had thought this, Nadia saw what Ciaran was thinking.

It worked.

Before the two enemy warriors saw 'Bixby' and

Nadia in the dark, Nadia felt energy drain from both her and Ciaran into the halberd.

The kilted Cameron guards promptly slumped down along the wooden wall, snoring as if they'd been asleep for an hour already.

Smiling at her, Ciaran quickly rolled the barrels over to protect the guards from being woken by the cows, then looked over toward the kitchen door.

No one was coming. The altercation had happened with barely a sound.

Squeezing her hand gently and with his mind full of glee, he opened the back gate and let them out. After closing it behind him, he started them toward Baltair and Eoin's hiding place at a quick walk. "We had best hurry, just in case someone coomes oot tae relieve themselves."

He had just started to speak, when suddenly she couldn't see him. Or herself. The two of them were invisible.

"How did ye dae that withoot me kenning, and how lang wull this last?" she asked him in her mind.

Holding her hand firmly, he broke them into a run along the beach between the two lochs toward the cover of the forest. "I hae na idea how lang 'twill last. Let us be oot o' sight from the gates when it wears off."

She ran with him, hand in hand on the firm wet sand. "But why did na I ken we were aboot tae be hidden?"

He gently squeezed her hand as they ran, and his mind caressed hers. "The halberd is evil, Nadia. I canna let ye feel its power."

She knew he was avoiding her question, and she wanted to press him for an answer, but then he filled their minds with such a compelling fantasy that she gave way to it as they ran, enjoying this look into the way his mind worked, his hopes and dreams.

TURNING TOWARD THE LOCH ON THEIR LEFT, Ciaran threw one arm around Nadia and raised the other to wave back-and-forth out into the waters, with his billowy sleeve flying.

Nadia was no longer able to hear his thoughts, and she squinted to see what he was waving at through the mist that enveloped the whole area, making it difficult to see the Cameron fortress or even the forest they had been running to.

She heard the sound of water lapping, but it was more rhythmic, as if several synchronized swimmers were all coming toward them. She peered through the mist, anxious to see. Why was he waving?

Her answer came in the form of a large serpent swimming across the water with its head pulled back to spit poison at her. She cringed into Ciaran, making his arms wrap around her all the more.

But he caressed her back and whispered in her ear softly, "Weesht, all well. 'Tis oor ain clan, the MacGregors, come tae be with us always."

Vaguely aware of her feet still running along the sandy beach but no longer wanting to pay that heed, Nadia looked out again into the mist of the loch toward what she thought was a monster.

Now, she saw a large Viking ship. The sea serpent was a decoration on the front of it, and the water lapping sounds were the oars sticking out of the sides. All her friends were on the ship, waving at her with smiles of welcome: Sarah was there, and Ellie, and even Kelsey.

"That's Kelsey's husband, Tavish MacGregor," Nadia said absentmindedly as she watched the kilted man lower a small boat and row it toward them by himself with room for the two of them in the back.

Ciaran cradled her in his arms. "Aye, Tavish is my cousin, and we all make a fine MacGregor clan."

Tavish smiled at them when he reached the

shore, jumping out of the boat and getting his boots wet, but holding firm to it and reaching out his hand to help her aboard. His handshake was friendly and welcoming.

Tavish rowed them to the Viking ship, telling them of the journey so far. "Ye are the last two we needed tae find, and 'tis sae glad we are that we did. We went and got Sarah and Meehall from the Murray castle, where they are well acclaimed and can gae back at any time, sae that's a place we may visit, aye?"

"Aye," Ciaran assured his cousin as he sat behind him in the rowboat with his arm around Nadia, who felt content to sit and listen, knowing she would soon see Sarah and Ellie.

They reached the ship and were hauled aboard to cheering from the rowing racks even as the oars took stroke again and rowed them away from the Cameron estate much too quickly in Nadia's opinion to be a natural thing. But why question this wondrous, perfect escape?

Sarah and Ellie were hugging Nadia while she looked around their new Viking ship home.

"Sae happy ye made it!"

Kilted men at the oars called out in greeting.

"Wull met, Ciaran! Nadia!"

"Now we are all, indeed, a clan!"

The captain stood at the tiller, an older man Nadia didn't recognize. He smiled at her and waved with a flounce of his own kilt, an outright MacGregor tartan, red and black and bold. "Hail, Nadia, and well come. I am Dall MacGregor, captain o' oor fair ship The Wanderer and chief o' oor small MacGregor clan. We dinna stand on ceremony, sae gae on below and make yourself at home. Quarters hae been prepared for ye and Ciaran, who I will marry as soon as we are safely away from Cameron lands."

Ciaran turned to her then, and when she met his eyes, they kissed in a way they hadn't yet done: empty of worry or fear, full of hope and plans.

Ellie opened a door that led to a wooden stair down into the hold. "'Tis this way. Ye wull love it."

Nadia followed with Ciaran directly behind her, and Tavish as well.

They were met at the bottom of the stair by a woman as handsome as Dall, and just as stately. "I'm Emily, Tavish and Tomas's mother. 'Tis sae relieved we are that ye made it. Allow me tae show ye tae yer cabin. Once ye are refreshed, I welcome ye at table for supper."

The hold held only cabins, nicely appointed.

There were silk and linen cushions and woolen blankets. Closets to hang up cloaks and extra skirts and shirts. Every couple had a door they could close to have privacy in their cabin — which was wondrous large, considering the size of the ship, plenty of room for two to comfortably stretch out or cuddle, as the case may be.

They were left alone there for a while to get used to the idea.

True to her word, Emily was standing in the hallway once they were hungry. "Sae glad I am tae hae all o' ye taegither. Ye canna ken." She hugged Ciaran in Nadia then, and although they had just met her, she felt motherly and comfortable and safe in a way that Nadia hadn't felt around anyone since she left home for Celtic.

Eoin and Baltair were already seated when Ciaran and Nadia sat, but then someone who looked a lot like Eoin and was every bit as big sat down at their table.

Eoin put his arm around the man and smiled. "This is my brother Gabriel, but he goes by Connell, as ye may wull understand, Gabriel being such a sissy name."

Connell socked Eoin in the arm, and then the two sat companionably while Eoin pointed out everyone else in the room. "Meehall and Sarah ye ken. That be Tomas and Amber. Jeffrey is at table with oor parents, Vange and Peadar. Lauren was invited, but she chose na tae come."

Connell took over. "Eoin's auld Jaelle also was invited and chose na tae come, but she lives in the time o' Hadrian's Wall, and we can visit there if we like, so that's well, aye?"

"Aye," Ciaran said heartily.

"There's Eoin," Ciaran said aloud, disrupting their daydream. The two of them had entered the cover of the trees where Eoin and Baltair sat, mounted and packed.

Collapsing with relief in the soft grass nearby, Nadia saw Ciaran and herself become visible again. Disturbed though she was at not being included in whatever it took to tell the halberd to stop hiding them, Nadia nevertheless took turns panting out their report to Eoin.

"The Camerons attack the Murrays tomorrow."

"We hae tae gae warn them."

"Tahra doesna ken time travel as yet."

"But she is dang a ritual tae get her power back."

"She has a history book from the future that says Ciaran's gang tae be instrumental in defending the Murrays in a grand battle."

"Tomorrow, they plan tae weaken the Murrays, sae that the battle, when it comes in a week or sae, wull hae a different outcome."

"We hae tae gae now."

Eoin cleared his throat. "Is your cover blown, Nadia?"

Ciaran's words swirled around Nadia's mind. "What can he mean?"

"Nay," she told them both. "The halberd made the guards sleep—"

"And we saw ye disappear!" said Baltair, who sat on his horse laughing.

Ciaran reached out a hand for Eoin to help him up on his horse behind him, thinking to Nadia "Yer welcome. I ken ye dinna want tae sit horse with Eoin."

"I thank ye," her mind told Ciaran's sincerely while she reached out to Baltair.

The smaller horseman was reaching down to her when Eoin spoke. "Nay. Nay, bide awhile. Gae back tae yer cover. Learn all ye can."

Ciaran's anger felt like hot lava bubbling up inside him, but it didn't burn her. "Nadia has risked her life for us already. Why would ye send her back intae that den o' thieves and worse, with that druid child in there looking for a sacrifice?"

Eoin looked regal on horseback. "Ye forget. We head intae an ambush we need tae warn them aboot. Two on two horses gae twice as fast as four on two horses." Eoin turned his horse.

Baltair gave Nadia a look of agreement with Eoin and turned to follow him.

Still full of rage, Ciaran called out after them, barely remembering to keep his voice down so as not to be heard from the Cameron house, "We wull follow ye afoot!"

Eoin stopped his horse so fast it stamped with indignation, swatting him with its tail. He reigned it even tighter, see-sawing the bit, and it quit. "The Camerons ride this way soon. They wull owertake ye. Nay, the least likely place for Nadia tae be discovered is in the Cameron house. Baltair and I will warn the Murrays. If we are in time and they fight off the Cameron attack, then when we return, I wull climb this tree and change its silhouette against the sky tae signal ye tae come oot. If I dinna dae sae by nightfall two days hence, then use the halberd and take Nadia tae her haime, for the Murrays are lost."

Finally, Ciaran calmed down. "Verra wull, but bring two more horses when ye return."

Eoin didn't quite roll his eyes. That wasn't his style, but he looked askance at Baltair, and the two of them took off in a cloud of dust. Very soon they were out of sight, up the mountain.

Ciaran was still holding her hand.

Wanting to restore a sense of urgency so that he held on, she said to him in her mind, "We had better get there before those two guards awake." She started to run.

Keeping hold of her hand, he drew her back into a walk, saying with amusement in his mind, "We can stroll a moment."

She gave him a mental hug of agreement, resisting the urge to squeeze his hand, but not quite succeeding.

He gently squeezed back, bathing her mind with admiration. "Ye are a verra brave lass, risking yer life for us when ye nearly lost it once afore."

Nadia was flattered, and since he was in her mind with her, she couldn't hide it, so she just let him feel it with her. "'Tis na bravery, but ainly my thirst for adventure and excitement. Till now, I didna ken how verra bored I had grown o' my duties as a clark at Celtic University."

The warmth and affection and reverence that built-up in their minds between them was too much to be contained just in their heads. Their bodies insisted upon that, clinging to each other in an embrace that both fulfilled the affection and made it grow more.

When her mouth met Ciaran's, she no longer felt weak in the least from the incident with the halberd. No, her strength was returning to her in a rush of elation as mouth-to-mouth with Ciaran, she felt finally whole and complete.

Parting from Ciaran was painful for her, once they had crept back inside the gates and he walked her to the kitchen door, waited while she went inside, then closed it. She lay down to feign sleep, but the next thing she knew, she was drifting off.

12

Ciaran had felt so strong, tasting Nadia's lips, he hadn't thought he would sleep. But the halberd had known better, hiding him as he lay down. He must have slept right through all the warriors leaving for battle, because he woke up in his empty stall, rested. The morning light came in through the cracks in the walls, and the horses were all gone. But the cows still mooed outside.

Ciaran got up and raked the stable, as that was Bixby's duty before he was allowed to go to the kitchen and get something to eat. While he worked, he remembered the elation of joining his lips to Nadia's. While they kissed, he hadn't missed the vigor the halberd drained from him. He hadn't felt any of the sadness present in his life —the loss of his family besides his cousins, Baltair and Eoin. While his lips caressed hers, he felt only joy. He was glad he kissed her. He needed some joy in his life.

When he went out into the stableyard with the intention of going to the kitchen for some food, Eimhir, the Cameron clan chief's pregnant wife, thrust two full pails of milk at him. "Take these intae the kitchen and coome back for the rest."

Ciaran couldn't hold both milk pails and his 'walking stick'. He stood there in the stableyard surrounded by cows and milkmaids, uncertain what to do.

Nadia came to his rescue, taking one of the pails from his hand and nodding her head toward the kitchen door while speaking to the other milkmaids. "I wull show him where tae put them." As she took up one of the pails and helped him carry the other so he could use his 'walking stick', she became close enough to say in his mind, "Think ye they warned the Murrays in time?"

"Aye," his mind told hers, "my cousins will na hae stopped till they arrived tae warn the Murrays."

"Put eh milk doon here," she said, indicating an area in the kitchen, and then once he had, "Come, let us gae and get the rest."

They stayed close together while they brought in three more pails of milk, but all they said to each other was a repetition of the wish that the Murrays had been warned in time. That their friends were safe. That their world was unchanged and whole.

When they came out again and there were no more full pails, Eimhir again spoke up. "Lame Bixby, help the lasses milk the coos, syne there are na horses for ye tae tend." With that, she went inside.

With a grin, Nadia snatched up a milk stool and brought it over to the cow behind her own milk stool, imagining the two of them back to back, still close enough to speak in their minds to each other.

He approved. No stranger to milking, having done it his whole childhood, he set to work, sending her his joy at being close together and speaking with her in their private mindscape. "Why did ye stow-away on oor apple wagon?" he asked her with genuine curiosity. "Why did ye want tae coome tae oor time?"

Amusingly, her first thought was a vision of him with his kilt flying up as he walked and his hair loose and long as he never had worn it. All of his muscles were exaggerated in her mind, and the smirk on his face was bigger than he ever remembered making it. She quickly suppressed that imagining, but it was too late. He had seen it. He knew she fancied him.

Unable to resist the lure of her attraction, he reached out with his mind and embraced her with more than just affection. Last night's kiss had roused... urges in him.

"Ciaran!" she reprimanded him, with a mindful of objections ranging from lack of privacy, to the need for vigilance here among their enemies, to a tiny sense of propriety.

But he could feel her own joy at their together-ness, there in her mind, and it was as great as his own, he was pleased to note.

While singing some unfamiliar tune with the other milkmaids on the outside, she turned serious on the inside, answering his questions. "At first, I came oot o' the need tae impress the Druids with a story oot o' history. But then there were the Camerons again, and I was trapped. I hae discovered more than I ever set oot tae."

Here, her memory of the druid child —who was there right now inside this very house— took over her consciousness. Tahra was storming down the cellar hallway and whipping a man to death.

She pushed down that memory. "And as I telt ye

last even, I hae often wished tae see faraway places, as long as I can remember."

He caressed her in his mind, attempting to settle both of their worries about what the druid child might do. While he did so, he told her in his mind, "I hae a longing for adventure as wull, and I share yer love o' discovering secrets and venturing tae unknown lands."

He was glad he had provided a distraction, because she latched onto it with gratitude. "Hae ye done much adventuring, then?"

"Aye, ye ken I wander with the Murray war party. We cover a lot o' land ower the course o' each year, ne'er settling in the same place twice. 'Tis a good life. And ye?"

"Aye. I coome from a land far away across the sea, a land called America—"

His amusement bubbled up inside their shared mind, giving them both a good bit of relief from their fear of Tahra. "Aye, I ken the new waurld."

"O' course ye dae. Wull, I coome from there, sae being anywhere here in Scotland is an adventure for me." Even as she thought this at him, though, she herself saw the lie to it. "At least, 'twas an adventure the first few months, working in the 'Druid Fortress', as ye think o' it."

Her image of the druid-run place where she worked and where Eoin was beholden —Celtic University, her mind called it— brought to his mind the dozens of huge greystone castles gathered together inside a stone wall that surrounded them in a way nothing from his experience ever had. It was like a large city, Aberdeen or Inverness, except the druids controlled the whole thing. And the place was... focused, all focused on the druids' purpose. He wondered if the druids controlled everything in the future.

"Nay, they dinna."

His immediate thought, uncontrolled and unbidden, was "Can she be certain?" He instantly denied this thought and mentally assured her he didna doubt her wisdom, it was just that a person could be mistaken.

Rather than argue, she brought him memories of everyday things in her life back home, away from Celtic University: skyscrapers, politicians, buses, movie stars, cars, charities, freeways, the peace corps, traffic jams, teachers and professors, supermarkets, televangelists, shopping malls, looking down from the sky in something called an airplane at night to see miles and miles of jewel-colored lights on the ground...

In her mind, it all made sense. And there was no trace of druidery involved in any of it.

It was so intense, the future, that for a moment, he had to pull away from her mind back into his own and try not to think about what he had seen.

""Tis sorry I am," she instantly said into his thoughts, almost as if they were his own thoughts, except hers were so feminine, so dainty. "Please dinna think I was trying tae overwhelm ye. I just want ye tae ken what I'm accustomed tae and why this is such an adventure for me."

"Aye, I dae see that this rough life is an adventure for ye. All right, I'm ready. Show me maire."

"I wull show ye how we spend most o' oor time."

Again, her mind had names for it all and an understanding of how it worked, so it wasn't as confusing as it might have been, but it was still overwhelming:

Television!

Computers!

Cell phones!

Something called the Internet that spanned the entire waurld!

He felt humbled by the vastness of her experience. Humbled and put to shame. "With all that tae explore, how can ye itch for adventure?"

"'Tis all in my mind, Ciaran, what I see on television and the computer and the cell phone and Internet. 'Tisna real. I canna taste it, smell it, or feel it. The Highlands are truly my most memorable experience e'er." Even as she said this, she was picturing him in her mind and thinking he was the most magnificent sight she'd ever seen.

IT WAS TIME TO TAKE ANOTHER LOAD OF MILK TO the kitchen, and Nadia got up and started the trip this time, smiling demurely when 'Bixby' got up to help her.

Mairee winked at Nadia when she saw them going to the kitchen again together.

Nadia winked back. After all, it was obvious she and Ciaran liked each other. There was no sense in denying it. That would look suspicious. And they were singing all three verses of the Rose Red rounds without her help now. She knew they were aiding the enemy, but she also knew they had little choice, and she was proud of them for learning the song so well.

Ciaran stayed close enough to her on the way into the kitchen and back out again so they could keep talking in their minds. "I dinna ken what else Eoin expects us tae discover. Mayhap for ye tae take anither gander at that book?"

Instead of answering him, she merely let her terror be felt. Amid that, anger bloomed. How dare he ask that of her? She fanned the flames of anger in his mental direction.

Having just set the pail of milk down in the kitchen, he put his hand up as if to fend off her fist. "I dinna mean for ye tae dae it. I only wonder what Eoin expects."

A few of the Cameron women in the kitchen looked askance at them, and he didn't seem to notice, so Nadia showed him their faces in her mind.

He sent her a big questioning feeling.

"We should na discuss this in here amidst sae many o' the enemy," she told him telepathically, pointedly leaving the house. "Ootside with the ither milkmaids, we wull be in maire sympathetic company, ye ken?"

"Aye," he sent to her mind apologetically, adding again emphatically, "I did na mean for ye tae dae it, Nadia. I was ainly asking what ye think Eoin expects us tae find oot."

As they moved their milking stools to the next set of cows, Nadia studied him for a moment to make sure he wasn't feigning ignorance to tease her. When she was satisfied he wasn't, she explained mentally, "Eoin does na expect us tae learn a thing, Ciaran. He ainly sent ye here because he kens ye wull na leave my side. And he ainly sent me here because he kens better than tae take me intae the fighting."

Realization dawned in his mind, and he sent out feelers to every area of her body —a tantalizing sensation— testing her reflexes in ways they had never been tested before.

When his words came to her mind, their tone was as if he had discovered she had never tasted milk. Or never walked barefoot on grass. Or never washed her face. "Ye hae na ever fought, hae ye?"

Words failed her, he was so shocked. She simply sent him the negative, the mental equivalent of shaking her head no.

He tentatively moved in for a mental embrace. "Ye dinna hae tae answer. I ken the truth o' it. I canna imagine it, but I ken 'tis true. I hae seen in yer memories that ye dinna fight battles by hand in yer time. On some o' yer 'TV shows' ye showed me, battles were fought at a distance using verra advanced firearms."

"I didna name firearms. We call them guns. Ye hae guns in this time?"

"Aye, we hae firearms in this time, but they are ainly used by the English. And those Scots who sail the seas in search o' others' property. Pirates, I believe ye call them. At any rate, we hae few people in this time who hae na fought. Ainly the truly infirm, like Bixby. How dae ye keep such a wondrous constitution, if na in training?"

Seeing herself in his mind's eye brought her understanding of his feelings to a whole new level. He admired her greatly, judging by the way her long hair flowed and glinted in the sunlight, not to mention the way she filled out her dress in all the right places. "Easier tae show ye, sae here." She took him along with her as she imagined herself doing the dance routine she'd been practicing in the hallway at Celtic while he and Eoin got the halberd. Her mind showed him all the kicks and the lunges, swaying along to the music it played for him.

THE MILKMAIDS HAD LONG SINCE GONE INTO THE kitchen to help prepare a feast for the returning warriors, and Ciaran knew Nadia was lingering out here with him on a thin excuse. Visiting with her in this manner for hours on end was the best time he'd ever had. It stirred him, made him want to take her by the hand and ask her to marry him right here and now,.

However, slowly at first, just a niggling worry, but then faster and with convicting certainty, the cold hard truth hit Ciaran in the gut, making him double over as he sat on his milking stool, missing the pail and shooting the milk into the ground with a hissing sound as its warmth hit the cold earth.

He couldn't ask Nadia to grow close to him and love him. All she would get was heartbreak. He needed to quit wooing her.

Shouts came from the distance.

"Hail the hoose!"

"Yer warriors are come haime!"

Eimhir opened the kitchen door and shooed out the milkmaids. "'Tis now safe tae let the coos oot. Come straight back in once ye hae finished, and help the wives prepare tae serve the warriors' feast."

There was a great hubbub as the milkmaids made their way through the crowd of moving cows to the front gate, pulled it open, and propped it with the barrels Ciaran had so conveniently left nearby. 'Bixby' helped them as best he could, having to lean on his stick.

And then they all went around to the other side

of the cows and shooed them out of the stableyard, making room for the horses and the men, who could be seen in the distance.

It wasn't long before the stableyard filled with stamping horses. But louder still was the shout that went up.

"Someone warnit the Murray clan!"

"They kenned we were coming!"

Every single hair on Ciaran's body stood up, and he moved close to Nadia, to protect her.

But no one even looked their way. Not while they were all bustling around in the stableyard, and not when they moved inside. Not even when Ruadh came in and addressed 'Bixby' with an air of self-importance.

"Wull lad, ye had a nice day off milking coos with the lasses, eh? Good, because ye hae yer night's work cut oot for ye, eh? All these horses tae tend tae." He slapped 'Bixby' on the back and ambled in through the kitchen toward the great hall to enjoy the feast the wives had prepared for the warriors.

Ciaran squeezed Nadia's hand one last time. When she looked over at him with a question in her eyes, he told her in his mind, "Thank ye for yer quick thinking. Even if calling me lame was a jest, methinks it may hae saved oor lives this day."

❧ 13 ❧

Nadia dreamed again that she was in the carving-decorated throne room beneath Dunskey Castle, wearing her threadbare 18th-century servant dress. Ciaran was here too, sprawled out on the throne next to hers in his kilt.

Kelsey stood across the room, wearing the white linen ceremonial robes of the druids. She had a garland of Rowan leaves in her hair, and a sprig of mistletoe hung from her white linen sash. Even though she stood and Nadia and Ciaran were on thrones, Kelsey's presence filled the room as if she owned the place. Which in more ways than one, she did.

And that was all. It was just the three of them.

Ciaran's thoughts were in her head without him visibly doing anything in the dream, just as they had been with the two of them in real life back in the Highlands in 1706. Thoughts only took an instant to fly back and forth between them.

"Sae good tae be away from the Camerons, even ainly in oor dreams. We could be in maire cheerful surroundings, though. This place is like a permanent funeral."

Nadia let him feel her amusement at his jest.

Kelsey gave no indication she had heard it.

Nadia enlarged her sense of wonder so that Ciaran could share in it. "Even here in the dream," she told him conspiratorially, "the halberd allows us tae speak in private, ainly the two o' us!"

"Aye," he thought back at her, "and 'tis wull. I dinna want that druid lass kenning all oor thoughts. She looks aboot tae blow the roof off the place, sae frustrated she is that she canna hear us as nay doubt she is accustomed tae in the realm o' dreams."

"Och, dinna fash. She is but Sarah's childhood friend who went tae Celtic and does the druids' bidding."

"Sae ye say," he thought at her with palpable doubt in his mind.

Nadia turned to Kelsey, speaking aloud. "Bring

Eoin, as wull! I'm dying tae hear if everyone's all right, and we need tae make sure he's bringing horses for us."

Kelsey barely acknowledged what Nadia had said, throwing her hand out in a dismissive gesture. "Eoin is busy with other things and canna be here."

Ciaran's thought on that was clear as day. "I dinna believe her."

Kelsey fastened her eyes on Nadia's for longer than was comfortable, then turned them on Ciaran by turns while she spoke. "Now, I hae disturbing news aboot Tahra's book. We researched it, combed all the records we hae here at Celtic. We foond nae mention o' Ciaran naywhere. The epic Cameron-Murray battle in this book is na mentioned, either. There be hints o' it, but it is na spoken o' in any historical texts, na even online. The ainly way tae ken for certain what happens is if we get oor hands on Tahra's book."

Kelsey looked like she was dismissing the idea of ever holding Tahra's book in her hands, but Nadia knew better. She couldn't say how, she just did. Kelsey was trying to manipulate them into getting Tahra's book. That's what was going on. She needed to bring Eoin here and tell them the truth and be straight with them, or Nadia wasn't going to help her—

"Halt, Nadia!" said Ciaran's frantic thoughts. "She is altogether tae powerful a person for ye tae confront. Play along with what she says. Please. She can hurt you. She can separate us. It is na worth it. Yer dignity is already safe and secure in my mind withoot that ye confront her, and it should be in yers as well. I'm begging ye, let this gae."

"There is na reason she canna bring Eoin intae this dream, and I dinna see how asking her tae dae sae should upset her."

"If ye ainly ask her, aye. Howsoever, 'twas na asking ye considered a moment hence. Ye were gaun'ae demand it o' her, and I was afeared o' her response tae that. I... I care for you deeply, Nadia. I dinna want any ill tae befall ye."

"Ye truly believe she would hurt me?"

"Aye, I dae."

"Dae ye think I could ask her again tae bring Eoin here?"

"Nay. I dinna think 'tis worth the risk."

"I had best say something now. 'Tis getting tae long syne last I spake."

"Aye. 'Twould dae na harm tae tell her what ye ken o' the book."

"Verra wull." Nadia raised her head up to Kelsey as if she'd just decided what to say. "Tahra had the book with her, the one time I saw her oot and aboot in the Cameron hoose. And when I went tae her quarters, she was in the bath, sae the book was on a pedestal therein. I suspect she never has that book far from her, but mayhap if Ciaran were tae create a distraction in the early morning while Tahra slept, and if it was enough o' a distraction, mind, mayhap Tahra would leave the book behind. I could slip intae her room and grab it."

Kelsey stared intently at Nadia a moment, then closed her eyes. When she opened them, she, Nadia, and Ciaran were in the hanging room at Cameron house, making friends with Mairee. Tahra's voice could be heard down the hall... Tahra walked by the open door, clutching the book... Tahra's voice was heard berating the man... The whipping... The dying man screaming... And then they were in Tahra's quarters, listening to Tahra's voice and the voices of her maidservants in the bathroom... And then they saw the book... And read it, slowly.

"What in the waurld is happening?" Ciaran's voice said in Nadia's head.

"Sarah telt me o' this," she told him silently in their shared thoughts. "Kelsey does na ainly coome intae dreams, she can alsae recall memories. Apparently she can fast-forward them, just like we can in the future, with things recorded on oor televisions."

"Yer lives are beyond my comprehension," he told her solemnly, looking at Kelsey with a combination of awe and terror.

The druidess had a faraway look on her chiseled features, her fair skin glowing with energy even in the dream as she worked some sort of magic that was incomprehensible to Nadia. Then she stopped abruptly, raised her eyes over to Ciaran, and spoke as if she were revealing the secret of the universe.

"Fire. Fire would get her oot o' bed in such a fright. Start it toward the north corner o' the barn sae that 'tis as far from her door as possible. Raise the alarm right away." She pivoted her head toward Nadia as if she were a cyborg. "Dinna gae up the stairs nor even leave the kitchen till ye hear the alarm. Ye must gae fast, and ye must gae furious. Nay hesitation. Say ye are gaun'ae put the fire oot. If ye are caught with the book, say ye rescued it for Tahra. And mean it."

With a decisive nod, Kelsey vanished.

Nadia was alone with Ciaran in the dream world, down inside the rune-carved great hall of the ancient Celtic seat of Scotland, beneath Dunskey Castle.

He got up off his throne and stepped toward her with a question in his eyes.

She got up as well, and in less than a second, they embraced.

Silently, she asked him, "Can ye start the fire she described?"

He clung to her, snuggling his face against hers. "Aye. I ken just how tae dae it."

She breathed in the earthy scent of him. "What alarm dae I listen for, sae that I ken when tae run up the stairs?"

He chuckled as he held her. "A bunch o' men yelling, starting with me."

"What wull ye yell?"

"Fire, fire, fire! What else would we yell?"

She laughed, and he joined in, their bodies rocking against each other in a very pleasing way. His mouth found hers again, and she threw herself into their kiss with abandon, letting joy fill her.

Abruptly, he pulled away. "I canna dae this."

He was gone, disappeared from the dream in a wink, as if no one had ever been there except her, alone in this cold damp basement throne room. It felt very lonely and empty without him there, and she stared around it, utterly confused, but also light-headed from the kiss.

Something must have happened back in the stable to distract him, she decided. Was it morning already? That must be it. She'd better go listen for his alarm.

❧ 14 ❧

It was still black night when Ciaran awoke, disoriented at first, but then remembering where he was, the Cameron fortress.

Bixby's orders were to tend to the horses, who had all just returned, sweaty and shivering. He must've fallen asleep too early. He got the 'walking stick' under him to help him up, in case Ruadh, his boss the stable head, appeared, then went to the stable door and looked out, noting how high the moon was in the sky, shining through the clouds. If the stars had been out, he would've had an even better idea how long he had until the sun came up. As it was, he figured he had three hours.

He didn't trust that druidess Kelsey. Nonetheless, he said a silent 'thank you' to her, for she must have woken him up from the dream, knowing how precarious his situation was here, how dangerous it would be for him to shirk Bixby's duty.

Bixby's 'walking stick' hummed in his hand and turned hot for a moment.

Shaking his head at the mystery of the thing and leaving the door open for the light, Ciaran went to the corner where the grooming items were kept and got the curry comb and the brushes, the rags, and the bucket for water. After he set them down on the shelf outside the first stall, he went out the gate to the loch and filled the bucket with cleaning water. Nodding to the watch as they passed by, he took the water to the first horse stall, then decided he needed to start the pretense now. Waiting, while more pleasant for him, would rouse suspicion.

Pretending the moonlight wasn't enough, he picked up the lantern and knocked on the kitchen door, holding it up.

Listening to the lasses bustle about inside with the breakfast preparations, he was hoping Nadia would answer, but of course it was Sorcha. She looked at him sternly, tapping her foot. "Why dae ye bother us? Ye ken we are busy."

'Bixby' held up the lantern, averting his face from looking at her in a way that she would find respectful. "I hae tae groom all the horses this night, and the moonlight is na longer enough."

Growling like a cat who's been put out of the house in the rain, she snatched the lantern from him and lit it in the fireplace. "Dinna make this a habit, ye hear?"

Conscious of his pretense at being lame Bixby, Ciaran gulped down an imaginary lump in his throat, trying to look put upon, when really he wanted to... Well, never mind. "Nay, I wull na make this a habit." He turned around, careful to lean on the walking stick and hold the lantern so it swayed as he limped away.

She must have noticed his difficulty, because she called out after him, "Hae a care with that lantern, mind!" The kitchen door slammed.

Feeling bad for what he had to do but also determined to do right by the horses first, Ciaran made his way back into the stable, limping and leaning heavily on his walking stick in case she opened the door again. He used a rag to wash the horse and dry it before using the curry comb and then the brushes on it so that its coat was clean and dry. And then he moved on to the next stall, and the next. By the time he'd finished grooming all the horses, the air had that chill which comes just before dawn.

It was time. After looking around at all the horses and calculating in his mind the place that would do the job, Ciaran set the lantern down in a corner and then pretended to trip over it, kicking the burning oil into a nearby pile of straw and falling down in the process. He shouted out in imaginary pain at having landed on his elbow while the fire caught well on the straw, then took his time getting up, using only one leg. Once it was burning brightly, he used the 'walking stick' to slowly reach the stable door and shout, "Fire, fire, fire!"

Noting with satisfaction that the fire was indeed going up toward Tahra's room, he limped over more quickly now and opened the first stall door, threw a rope around the horse's head, limped out into the stableyard leaning heavily on the 'walking stick,' and yelled out "Fire, fire, fire!" again when he released the horse. On to the next horse he went, and the next, and the next. When he came to the fifth stall with his stick and his rope, Cameron men came rushing to put the fire out, cursing him as they did so.

"Ye had tae hae a lantern!"

"Get the horses oot!"

Ciaran didn't have to be told to get the horses out. He had considered letting them out into the stableyard before he set the fire, but of course that would've given him away. No, he'd had to do things this way, and so he threw himself into getting them out of the burning stable into the yard. He was close to opening the gate and letting them out into the wild, but the Cameron men were doing a good job getting the fire out. Perhaps too good.

No, the distraction served its purpose. Tahra came running out of the house in her chemise. Clutching the bedclothes around her with both hands, hair all disheveled and smelling of smoke, she stormed at Ruadh, yelling, "Punish that clumsy oaf who started the fire!"

Ruadh fetched a switch, and the older man's look said to 'Bixby,' "I gave ye a chance, and look how ye repay me. I will na gae easy on ye because o' yer lame leg, either. Ye hae this coming, and wull ye ken sae. But I wull spare yer life, sae dinna ye fash for it. Grit yer teeth, for 'tis coming."

Looking all around for a supportive face and finding none more so than Ruadh, 'Bixby' quickly tucked his walking stick through the front of his belt, holding it there as if his life depended on it.

Amid the horses, who were skittish from the fire and running about this way and that in the stable-yard, two Cameron men took Bixby by the elbows and carried him to the front gate, pushed the front of him till he was leaning on it with both hands, then pulled his shirt up to expose the skin of his back.

Anxious for Nadia's safety, Ciaran looked to see if the fire was under control. It was almost out, which relieved him.

Ruadh gave him a scant nod in agreement before he brought the switch down on Ciaran's back. In all, he gave him 30 lashes.

It was painful, but nothing Ciaran couldn't handle. 'Bixby,' on the other hand, screamed out in pain at each and every lash.

Ruadh turned to see if the druid child's demand for justice was satisfied, but she was overseeing the fire dousing with hollered commands.

However, the Cameron warriors knew what they were doing and showed a great deal more sense, in Ciaran's opinion. "The cripple has been punishit. Good with the horses, is he. We could use his help getting them back in the stable."

Tahra turned steely eyes on 'Bixby.'

He lowered his head as if ashamed, hoping that even up close like this, she wouldn't recognize the man who had helped rescue her ritual sacrificial maidens barely a week ago.

She didn't. "Aye, he wull get all the horses back in the stable, and then he will be jailed and chained until I deem he has been punishit enough."

The two Cameron men let go of Bixby and lowered his shirt back down.

'Bixby' took his walking stick out of his belt and went to the stable and got the lead rope.

Ruadh accompanied him, hollering curses at him aloud, but breathing out softly, "I wull see tae it ye are na doon there ower long. I wull tell her I need yer help."

"I thank ye," was all Ciaran said, thinking anything more would have ruined the simple-minded Bixby character he was playacting.

Anyway, he held no resentment at being told to put the horses back in the stable. They were still skittish from the smoke even though the fire was out and likely to injure each other. They would be much calmer in their familiar stalls. He found it soothing, putting the rope over each one's head and calmly leading it back into the stable. They trusted him, horses and cattle. He was glad he had taken the time to relieve them all of their sweat before beginning the ruse which got Tahra out of her room.

All he hoped now was that it had been worth it.

The same two men who had held him while he was switched took his arms again and carried him down the stairs into the dungeon.

Just before they did, he desperately tucked his 'walking stick' through his belt again.

This time, it promptly vanished from view, draining him of strength.

He wondered if he would need that strength while they chained him to the wall, locked the door to his cell, and walked up the stairs, laughing together.

Alone, he felt the pain of his bloody back against the wooden wall of the dungeon cell, right through his shirt. He arched his back to avoid that, but he could feel his muscles cramping.

He didn't know how long he had stood there before he heard a noise on the stairs and felt some anxiety. Was it the Cameron men come to torture him? He hadn't thought they looked especially resentful of him, but who knew what that druid child Tahra might make them do.

And then he relaxed when Nadia's soft whisper came lilting down the stairs to him.

"Bixby? Bixby, are ye doon here?"

He didn't answer. He didn't want her to see him like this.

But she came down anyway and put her hands on the bars in the window of his cell door, looking at him with stricken eyes full of tears. "What hae they done tae ye?"

All he could think for a solid minute was she wasn't close enough! He couldn't have the halberd take them out of this place, let alone hear her thoughts or show her silently what he was thinking. There was a space under the door, but it wasn't quite large enough for her to squeeze through.

"Dinna fash upon me," he told her. "'Tis na what I'm afashit aboot." He lowered his whisper till it was barely audible. "Did ye get it?"

She swallowed and wiped her tears, which was pointless, because she kept shedding more. "Aye," she whispered, "I got it."

"Slide it under the door tae me." He held her gaze and used his eyes to plead that she understand. "Ye canna be caught with it."

Her eyes searched the cell and then grew round with panic. She frantically shook her head no.

He willed the walking stick to show itself to her, and it did. He looked at her with significance in his eyes, praying that she understood.

She put a tentative hand on a bundle that was tied under one of her skirts. "It wull hide it?"

"Aye," he rushed to assure her. "Ye ainly need slide it close enough."

She looked over her shoulder at the top of the stairs, then put her hand on the bundle again tentatively, freezing there with indecision.

"Dinna bring trouble doon upon yer ain head," he whispered to her desperately. "Ye hae tae stay clear o' trouble till I get released," he pled, his eyes beseeching her.

She swallowed and nodded ever so slightly, then looked again over her shoulder before taking the book out from under her skirts, kneeling down, and quickly sliding it under the door toward him in tearful torment at the risk they were taking, having the book out in the open.

He smiled at her and nodded his thanks at her trusting him.

But something was wrong. Her eyes and mouth opened wide. She gasped in panic. Whatever could be the matter?

He looked down where she was looking and saw that the book had caught on a stone midway between them.

She was sobbing now, the racking sobs of the

heartbroken. "Nay, och, nay, nay, nay, nay, nay. What wull we dae?"

What would they do, indeed?

"Ye must gae, Nadia. Gae, afore ye are caught doon here!"

❧ 15 ❧

Ciaran put into his voice every bit of pleading he could, desperate for Nadia not to get caught even more than he worried for his own life.

As soon as he thought his own life was in danger, the book slid all on its own the rest of the way to the walking stick, up the stick, and into his belt with it. He felt strength drain from him, the book vanished, and he passed out.

❧

WITH TREPIDATION, NADIA WENT BACK upstairs. The wives were making cheese out of all the milk that hadn't been used in cooking yesterday's feast. They had heated it last night and added a bit of existing cheese, and now they were straining the curds. She didn't relish the thought of helping with that. Their cheese was smelly. She preferred milder cheeses that didn't stink so much.

But as soon as Nadia hit the top step, a crying Mairee who looked so distraught Nadia almost didn't recognize her ran over and grabbed her by the wrist and pulled her down the hall into the laundry room. After taking great care to close the door quietly behind them, she then pulled Nadia behind one of the washtubs, ducking down so they would be hidden if anyone opened the door.

Nadia didn't struggle. Mairee was a friend. But she did ask, "What's gang on?"

The air rushing through half a dozen pairs of frightened female lips shushed her.

"Shhhhhhhhh!"

Nadia looked, and the other washerwomen / milkmaids peered at her in the darkness from behind the other wash bins.

Barely audible and holding Nadia down behind the wash tubs with shaking hands, Mairee said to her through tears, "Tahra is oot for blood."

Sorcha took over when Mairee was sobbing too much to speak. "She's gang on and on aboot that book she always has with her. Misplaced it, she has, and she's blaming everyone but herself. Mairee has been sae fashit aboot ye. Praise be tae God she at last has found ye."

Nadia turned a grateful face to her friend, though inside she was trembling with guilt over putting them all in danger by taking the book. "I thank ye, Mairee, for taking the tyme tae bring me in here."

Mairee nodded, but instead of saying anything, she just bowed her head and put her finger over her lips.

Nadia nodded as well, and they all crouched there, silent and sobbing, frozen in terror while outside the sanctuary of the laundry room they heard yelling, pots and pans hitting the floor, and shrieks of fear. They winced at every crash, gasped at every scream, and ducked lower every time footfalls came down the hall toward them.

Tahra drove all this, raging at everyone.

"A spy lurks among us!"

"Someone telt the Murrays o' oor ambush and ruinit my plan!"

It went on and on, until Nadia's hands ached from their white-knuckled hold on the rim of the wash basin. And then she heard a particularly loud scream, followed by the druid child uttering words Nadia couldn't ignore.

"If ye return my book tae me now, Boisil here will be spared. But if I dinna hae my book in my hand by the time I count fifty, he wull die. One... Two... Three..."

Bile came up Nadia's throat into her mouth, and she let go of the wash tub. A man was going to die because of her, because of something she had done.

Giving her loyal women a pained face that did its best to say she really wanted to stay in this room and be safe but she just had to leave, Nadia quietly left and snuck back down into the dungeon. At Ciaran's cell door, she grabbed onto the bars and put her face right up against them so that he could see her and know she'd been crying and was afraid.

His face became stricken, and he struggled violently with the chains that bound him. "What's the matter? Is the hoose under attack?"

Nadia shook her head furiously, saying more to the halberd than to him, "Nay, yer life is na in danger."

He stopped struggling with his chains, to her immense relief. She couldn't bear to think what Tahra would do to him if he were found loose in the house right now. She knew he didn't think there was enough juice in him and her and the halberd to get them safely away from here after freeing him from his chains, or he would have done so earlier, instead of just making the book disappear.

Sighing with relief that he wasn't going to break free and rush upstairs to be killed, she rushed to explain in the barest whisper what had to be done. "Nay, naught o' the sort. But Tahra's gaun'ae kill Boisil unless I return the book tae her now, sae give it tae me." She bent down and reached her hands out under the door, ready for him to have the halberd slide the book back to her.

"Ye ken it does na work this way," he said to her with that same resolve in his voice.

What was he talking about? She stood and fixed her eyes on his, pleading with him. "She's gaun'ae kill him!"

"It ainly works if some aught wull kill me," he reminded her.

Oh no. He was right. "We hae tae convince it ye wull be kilt, then," she insisted.

Puzzlingly, Ciaran's face filled with sympathy for her, but he hardened it into resolve. "Nay, Nadia. The druid child's lack o' that book wull save thousands o' lives, and besides, ye canna trust her tae keep her word. She is devious and cunning.

Gae and find a hiding place tae bide in till I am freed. The man's blood is on her hands, 'tis na on yers."

As he spoke, her determination to give the book back slowly drained away. He was right. More to herself than to Ciaran, she whispered, "Tahra must hae reached fifty by now anyway." She wanted to argue, but it wouldn't do to cause Ciaran any more anguish than he already was in.

His eyes were blackened and his raw back pulled away from the wood behind him.

She gave him a pained smile and then went back up the stairs to the laundry room to hide.

HER NEW LOYAL FRIENDS ALL WELCOMED HER with grimacing smiles.

But after a short while, Sorcha stood up and let go of her white-knuckled hold on the wash bin. "We hae tae gae back tae oor duties, afore we are sorely missed and someone decides tae punish us." With that, she calmly walked to the door, opened it, and left, not quite closing it behind her.

Mairee looked at Nadia for her reaction.

Nadia nodded and got up as well. "Ye canna

fault her reasoning. Aye, we must gae back tae oor duties."

They all left the washing room together and headed for the kitchen, which was surprisingly in the same shape as when Nadia had passed through earlier, with several of the wives straining the curds from the whey. The pots and pans once more hung from a rack by the fireplace.

Nadia went up to the women who were curding. "Show me how ye dae this here."

Later that evening, Nadia was sent out into the stableyard with a bag of vegetable peelings and scraps from the supper trays. She was busy feeding them to the chickens when she glanced up toward Eoin's tree, hoping to see it changed. It hadn't been, and she was horrified by the site of a man's charred body hanging on a pike by the front gate.

❧

IT WAS A NIGHTMARE, THIS CURSED WAR AXE. Tightly held against him as it was by his belt, it fed images into Ciaran's mind, images and sounds of the horror happening in the house and stableyard above.

Punctuated by the halberd's joyful song of fighting lust, Ciaran saw the whole thing: Tahra torturing the servant for information on where her book was. The servant begging and swearing it wasn't him who took it. Tahra having no mercy. Tahra tying the man to a stake in the stableyard, piling hay and wood around him, and burning the man alive in front of the clan. It was a warning, she explained. This was what happened to those who betrayed her.

Ciaran's arms and legs were shackled, so he drew in his belly as far as he could, trying to get the halberd to fall to the floor, away from him. It didn't budge, even though it should have. It was thinner than the book. The book should have stayed and allowed the halberd to slip away from him. Both stayed put.

The cursed halberd held such sway over him that he wasn't sure he could cast it aside even if he had the use of his limbs. He should have taken heed of Eoin's warning, should have noted the gloves his cousin wore to handle it. Should have cast it aside while he still could. Should have buried it like the druids had told Eoin would be best.

❧ 16 ❧

Ciaran hadn't expected to sleep, but he awoke to the sound of footsteps coming down the stairs into the dank smelly basement. Every muscle in his body ached from standing for so long, and he feared for Nadia. Was she safe? Much as he wished it weren't, the halberd disguised as walking stick was firmly in place in his belt.

It was the two men who had brought him down here the night before, and they cheerfully unlocked his cell door and came in, bustling about unlocking his shackles. "Ye hae been chosen tae gae with Tahra tae help her. 'Tis a great honor. Ye should be proud."

That was a lie, of course. Anyone 'helping' her would be on either end of the sacrifice needed to regain her dark magic. Now he was glad he still had the halberd. We would see who was going to be the sacrifice.

The men took him up the stairs, waited while he ate some bread and cheese, and even took him into the laundry room, saying, "Wash yerself. Ye hae tae ride with us, and ye smell like the devil."

It was tempting to leave himself smelling that way, but in truth he couldn't stand the smell of himself either. So he dropped his kilt, took off his boots, gripped the book and his 'walking stick' firmly in one hand, and climbed naked into one of the washtubs. The water was passable tepid, not as cold as he feared, and he ducked under and got his hair wet, even grabbed some soap and washed the smelliest parts of him before getting out and drying off with some linen someone had conveniently left there.

Feeling refreshed, he dressed, stuffed the book back into his belt, and used the 'walking stick' to limp back out into the hallway. He was all smiles until they took him through the yard toward the stable and he saw the wagonful of milkmaids and a few male servants. Nadia was among them. Furthermore, she was seated as far in front of the wagon as she could get, right behind the driver. Even if he ran to her right now, she was too high up. There was no way to get close enough to speak into her mind, let alone have the halberd take her away to safety.

Nadia smiled at him and waved, happy to see him.

With his eyes and his facial expression, he tried to show her what he was thinking —that as soon as they were away from the Cameron fortress, she should jump out of the wagon and run to him.

She clearly had been expecting him to greet her, because doubt now filled her eyes.

Her doubt made his heart ache, so he pushed down the desperation he felt at knowing it would be difficult to get her out of this situation. All he let show on his face was his love for her.

She smiled, lighting up her face like the sun when it comes out of the cloudy sky over a meadow full of flowers.

Tahra and a dozen warriors rode out of the stable. Ruadh was one of them, and he reached down and pulled 'Bixby' up behind him, nodding at the two Cameron men who had gotten him from the dungeon, who went into the stable and also came out on horseback. The horses took the lead, and the wagon followed behind as they rode out the gate, down the narrow space between the two lochs, and into the forest.

"Some call the place we gae tae Fae Wood," Ruadh told 'Bixby' as they rode. "Many will na enter it, afeared o' being tricked by the faeries."

This barely registered on Ciaran's thinking. Ruadh nattered on, and Ciaran was grateful for his friendliness, but he was desperate to get Nadia away from the druid child.

When they had been riding along a seldom-used road through the forest for several hours, the horses slowed to a stop amid the trees and allowed the wagon to catch up. Provisions were taken from the wagon and passed around. Everyone ate smoked deer and bread. The horses were watered from a nearby stream and given free rein to eat the delicate grass that grew just off the road.

These stops were not frequent, but they happened often enough to get Ciaran's hopes up. Every time those on horseback drew close to the wagon, Ciaran prayed that Ruadh would choose to go over on the side where Nadia was, close enough so that he could use the halberd to take her away.

It was on the tip of his tongue, one of those times, to ask Ruadh to go on her side of the wagon. But the instant he opened his mouth to say something, Ruadh clasped forearms with one of the other Camerons, smiling and jesting while people waited in the wagon. These warriors had to know why the milkmaids were along.

Ciaran would wait for his chance. Finally, he saw it coming.

Everyone had stopped once more. Tahra and her first man were discussing where they should stop for the night. Ruadh was pulling up beside the wagon on Nadia's side to take some water the wagon driver was offering him.

Ciaran knew he would only have the amount of time it took for Ruadh to drink. He met eyes with Nadia and let his determination show on his face and pleading with her to stay put, to be ready.

Understanding showed on her face, and she edged a little closer to the side of the wagon, also closer to him.

Up at the front of the party, Tahra whirled her horse around, demanding, "Everyone, follow me!"

Everyone did, of course. Ruadh responded immediately, turning their horse and speeding away from Nadia.

Ciaran cursed himself. Why hadn't he listened to his instincts before? He should have wished the halberd would take them away to safety when Eoin and Baltair refused to take the two of them back to Murray camp. Failing that, he could have grabbed

Nadia and whisked her away before he got shackled.

Why had he consented to the plan of her taking this accursed book? The halberd had claimed his life now, changing his fate, so what did it matter what the book said would happen to him? It wouldn't now be true, anyway.

Ruadh stopped with all the other warriors. This time, instead of waiting for the wagon, he dismounted and nodded to 'Bixby' to do the same. "There is na room for all the servants tae sleep in the wagon, ye ken, sae some o' ye wull be sleeping under it."

Ciaran gave Ruadh an inquisitive look. "I—"

Hints of sympathy came into Ruadh's eyes.

Before the man could say anything, the same two Cameron men who had brought Bixby up from the dungeon appeared, taking Bixby by either hand and leading him gruffly away.

One of them said over his shoulder, "Ye are tae soft, man."

The other spat, then looked at Ruadh and away.

But Ciaran's heart was eased. These two ruffians were not going toward the wagon, where they might do harm to Nadia. No, instead they were going up the nearby hill.

They bound 'Bixby's hands together behind him, pushed him over on his side to the ground, bound his ankles together, and shoved him under the bushes, apparently to spend the night. Then they walked away laughing with their kilts bouncing at every scornful step.

Ciaran waited there in the darkness and discomfort for food to be brought, but it never was. He heard them all laughing and joking, then finally singing around the fire, so he knew they were getting food.

How was Nadia faring? Did they feed her? He didn't hear any screaming or crying, so at least they weren't mistreating her or the other lasses.

He was uncomfortable and worried. There was no way he could sleep lying here on the cold earth with his hands bound so tightly behind him.

The Cameron men would get what they had coming. He had only to bide his time until they were all asleep, full of ale and comfortable around their fire.

Once all the sounds had died away and even the fire crackling had stopped, he thought about the sacrifice that was sure to come and how he was no doubt part of it. Otherwise, why had they tied him up?

As soon as he thought of his life being threat-ened, he thought of the most logical thing that could be done to help save him.

The leather thongs that tied his arms and his ankles dissolved.

He was free. Only a small amount of strength had drained from him, so he was confident he would be able to get Nadia away from here. All he had to do was get close enough to touch her, and they would be safely away.

❦ 17 ❦

Even here in a dream, the cold earth chilled Nadia through the thin plaid blanket she'd been given to lie down on under the wagon. She knew she was dreaming, because as she sang, she couldn't hear the audience with her ears, only with her mind. If only it were possible to know, in real life, how much they loved her song just like she knew they did in her dream. She was singing one of her favorites:

> If I should enter intae yer bower,
> I am na earthly man;
> And should I kiss yer rosy lips,
> Yer days would na be lang.

My bones are buried in yon kirk-yard,
Afar beyond the sea;
And 'tis but my spirit, Margaret,
That's now speaking tae thee.

She stretchit oot her lily hand,
And fought tae dae her best,
Here be yer faith and troth, Willie;
God send yer soul tae rest.

Now she had kilted her robes of green
A piece below her knee,
And all the live-lang winter night,
The dead corpse followed she.

Be there room tae spare at yer head, Willie,
Or any room at yer feet?
Or any room at yer side, Willie,

Wherein a lass may creep?

There is na room at my head, Margaret;
There is na room at my feet;
There is na room at my side, Margaret;
My coffin's made sae meet.
https://www.youtube.com/watch?
v=UGFSJ5rdWuU
(YouTube: Nuala Honan - Lady Margaret and Sweet
William - Traditional)

SHE LOOKED FOR KELSEY. THE DRUID HAD TO BE here if this wasn't really a dream but a sleeping reality where someone else could be aware of her. This smacked of Kelsey.

But Nadia's druid coworker was nowhere about.

Oh, how the audience loved Nadia, singing along as one voice, they urged her on to more, saying with their yearning how they loved the sound of her voice, how much they enjoyed how happy she was when she sang.

She came to the end of that ballad and was thinking what song she should sing next when she realized why the audience were speaking with one voice.

This wasn't an anonymous audience, it was Ciaran.

She wasn't dreaming, she was slowly waking up while communing with him once more, in their minds.

His deliberate thought to her re-enforced this realization. "'Tis sae glad I am that all is wull with ye."

"Nay more glad than I am tae see ye are wull. When they took ye away, I—"

He put his physical hand gently over her lips. "Dinna fash upon it. We are taegither now. But Tahra plans tae sacrifice all the servants sae she can hae her magic anew. We must gae." He tried to pull her up, and he imagined she would grab his hand and let him lead her away on foot.

She resisted him.

He let go of her hand immediately, but he lowered himself to her side once more, radiating baffled hurt while still desperate for her to follow him away from the Cameron camp.

She gently took his hand and let him feel the love she yet had for him, saying silently in their still mingled minds, "I'm afeared tae gae on foot. If they catch us, 'tis sure they are tae kill us." She tried not to imagine what that would be like, but her mind went with it, showing him the Cameron warriors lopping off their heads.

He didn't pull her this time, but he imagined her getting up on her own, and he prepared to do the same. "Being caught and killed while we run is less certain than what they plan for the morrow, Nadia. We must leave."

Giving him a new scenario to look at, she said to him in their minds, "Use the halberd! Take us clean away from here, ower tae Murray camp sae we can bring help and rescue Mairee and the others. They hae been sae welcoming tae me, I feel they are like sisters." She said it gently, giving him the benefit of the doubt. But had he forgotten about the halberd? He had it with him, disguised as Bixby's walking stick.

Disappointment emanated from him. "Be assured that I tried tae will us away with the halberd the moment I first arrived by yer side and touched yer fair skin. Howsoever, the cursed thing has power ower me now. Unable am I tae exert my will ower it betimes, and I canna lay it doon." A ray of hope entered his mind. "If we gae tae sleep, can ye summon yer friend Kelsey intae oor dreams, sae we can ask her tae get us away?"

It was her turn to emanate disappointment, but she fought that feeling, trying instead to push into his heart some of the faith she had in his fighting prowess. "Nay, it does na work that way. I canna summon Kelsey. Ainly she can create such a dream."

To her surprise, her faith in his fighting skills made him ashamed. Even as he flexed his muscles to show that indeed he was up to the task. "Nadia, Tahra wull na win. I wull use the halberd tae cut her doon. Howsoever, the thing is accursit. I kenned it was. Eoin wore gloves when he held it, and he did warn me na tae use it. But I defied him. It wull make for me an early death, any time now."

What? She couldn't have heard that correctly! An early death? Any time now?

The sadness in his mind told her she had heard right, though. And he wasn't sad for himself, but rather for the time he would lose with her.

Even as this endeared him to her all the more, Nadia's heart broke. All the hope she had stored up for a life with him, children with him, drained out of her. She was hollow, hopeless.

He felt it, and he embraced her heart with his.

Right. He was still here with her. He deserved

better than her sadness. Nadia gave in to his embrace and willed Ciaran to feel all the love she had for him, all her yearning to have him with her always. Tears burst from her eyes, and she started sobbing, trying her best to do it silently and not wake the others, unable to trust them not to give him away to the Cameron warriors.

He gathered her into his physical arms and held her close, using his elbows to rock her softly in a soothing motion and speaking to her in their shared consciousness. "Nadia, dinna cry for me. I resigned myself tae an early grave days hence. Allow me tae see ye safe." Again, he imagined her getting up and taking his hand and allowing him to lead her away.

Quietly, in their minds, she told him, "I wull na hae ye blaming yerself fer my death, sae I wull na flee, lest they catch me. We love each other, sae let us be together as long as we can. If 'tis ainly this one night, then sae let it be. Make the best o' it, the time we hae here under the stars in the Fae Wood, where anything is possible."

An idea formed in his mind like a seed sprouting, slowly at first, but growing greener and taller every moment. "We bide in the Fae Wood," he thought at her, "surrounded by the faeries, magical creatures who may indeed hae what it takes tae save us." He thought back in his mind to his childhood and summoned a song his mother had taught him about the faeries.

...What makes you pull the poison rose?
What makes you break the tree?
What makes you harm the little babe
That I have got with thee?

Oh I will pull the rose, Tam Lin
I will break the tree
But I'll not bear the little babe
That you have got with me

If he but were a gentle man
And not a wild shade
I'd rock him all the winter's night
And all the summer's day...
https://www.youtube.com/watch?
v=c3yTEUnyYDA
(YouTube: Folk Alley Sessions: Anaïs Mitchell &
Jefferson Hamer - "Tam Lin (Child 39)")

In their mingled minds, she joined in with him singing. The song was a familiar one, and they sang the many verses together.

It was an odd plan his mind had formed, singing about the fae to make them appear, but If druids could visit them in their dreams and hear their thoughts, then how much more likely the unearthly Fae could hear their thoughts in real life within the Fae Wood, being far more magical?

After a time, she thought she heard the Fae answer. Their musical voices had an ethereal beauty, sounding like an orchestra made entirely of stringed instruments not quite loud enough for her to make out the words. Was it real, or was she imagining it?

"Aye, 'tis real," said Ciaran's thoughts. "That be the fae. Their answer grows stronger. Listen, and soon we wull hear."

Hope filled them both as they lay in the darkness under the wagon, holding each other close and listening for the song of the faeries. Hope lent an eerie beauty to the moonlight streaming through the clouds and trees to land on the grass. It made the cold air feel bracing, rather than deadly.

When the faerie song grew loud enough for them to discern, hope fled. "Nay," sang the faeries in their wispy melodic voices. "We wull ne'er help the likes o' ye! Ye are na worthy, and furthermaire, ye hae na suitable sacrifice in yer power tae give."

Faerie laughter erupted nearby. Cacophonous as a room full of toddlers singing out of tune, it grew louder and louder, until Nadia knew the fae were very close.

And then someone else caught the faeries' attention. Too far away for words to come clearly, Tahra called out to the fae with a surprised but eager voice.

Nadia was gripped by fear.

Ciaran was as well, but he fought through it and articulated thoughts to her, once more full of shame. "Nadia, forgive me. I brought them upon us!" He withdrew his arms from around her, imagining himself flat on his belly in front of her feet while she looked down on him with a grim frown.

She threw her own arms around him, willing him to feel all her love, assuring him it had not diminished one bit. She imagined herself lying next to him, just as they were, fusing the mental and the physical together into a strong reality as she hugged him tight in both realms, crooning to him in her mind silently, "I love ye, I love ye, I love ye with all my heart."

He struggled in her arms, reverting to the image of the two of them getting up and running.

She quickly doused that idea, showing him the

crowd of faeries nearby as best she could imagine them, waiting for a tasty sacrifice the druid child would be all too happy to give them tonight, rather than in the morning. She insisted again she would not be a source of grief to him. She would not allow him to lead her to Tahra and the faeries. "Let them come take us," she told him firmly, "but I will na gae tae them."

He quit trying to get her to run, but he still wasn't relaxing in her arms.

She changed the subject. "How did ye get here under this wagon, anyway? They canna hae left ye tae wander the camp as ye wulled." She imagined just that, them all going off to their fire together to carouse and have fun and just leaving addlepated lame Bixby standing there by himself, unguarded. She added a touch of laughter.

Slowly, her good humor ate through his anxiety until it was gone. Hope bloomed in him once more, and with it the ability to accept her affection, and to return it. He did so warmly, renewing their embrace both physically and mentally. "They did na. They bound me and shoved me under a bush withoot even a plaid tae lie on, 'twixt me and the damp earth."

She kissed his cheek as she lay there in his arms. "Sae how did ye get the bonds untied?"

Excitement bloomed in Ciaran, making him perk up like a kitten who's seen a string dragged by his face. "'Twas the halberd. I willed the halberd tae dissolve my leather bonds."

She let the excitement bloom in her as well, but she imagined herself more like a kitten who sees food coming and jumps up to go where it will be. "Sae ye can get the halberd tae dae some aught, just na whisk ye away."

"Aye," he said, his excitement growing. "Aye, that I can."

in her mind, she sat back and looked up at him with pride, like the kitten who saw another kitten kill a mouse.

They shared all the love they felt for each other in a dizzying dance of happiness and hope regained.

18

Ciaran awoke to the rude shoving and voices of the Cameron men. "Get yer sorry selves up and intae the wagon. Tahra wull hae yer hide if ye dinna."

He wanted to call their bluff. Tahra planned to kill them all in her ritual, and these men had to know that. But they were shoving Nadia as well. He couldn't bear to be the cause of harm to her at their hands, so he took out his walking stick, kept quiet, and limped in between her and them so that only he would get pushed and shoved.

'Attack them!' the warrior in him screamed.

''Tis twelve on one,' he told his inner warrior, 'and pinned against the wagon am I.'

This was not the time. It would come, he knew it,

and so he shielded Nadia long enough for her to get in the wagon, and then he held fast to his walking stick and got on the wagon with her, making sure to crawl in close to her so that the two of them would be able to speak in their thoughts.

She was worried for him. "Dinna fight them, Ciaran. Gae where they tell ye, for my sake."

"I wull for now, but be on yer watch. Ye must away at the first chance."

"I wull watch for my chance, but ye must come along."

He couldn't bear to voice his plans to her, not even silently in their minds. So he showed her, letting it play out in his musings like a daydream. Sometimes, he ran at Tahra and used the halberd to chop the druid child in half. Other times, he stabbed her in the back.

Once everyone was underway again, Sorcha passed him a large skin of something warm with a look of appreciation. "'Tis beef broth."

He passed it first to Nadia and let her drink her fill before taking his and passing the now empty skin back.

Nadia kept showing him her own daydreams, which always had the two of them leaving together. "We canna allow Tahra tae perform the ritual,"

Nadia admitted to him in her mind. "We must find a way tae stop it, aye. Howsoever, we hae the book now, and sae ye must na throw yer ownself away. We wull stop her."

"We wull," he told her, but he knew she could hear his true thoughts: I wull attack Tahra and kill her the first time I get the slightest chance, and I dinna mind what happens tae me.

"Ye dinna need tae gae alone," she told him, trying a different tack. "Dinna keep from telling me how the rest o' us can help." She imagined all sorts of impractical helps. The milkmaids all cracking the warriors over the head with porcelain vases was his favorite.

The motion of the wagon was hypnotic, and he must've passed a terrible night. Even though he was greatly afeared for everyone's safety and determined to stop Tahra's ritual before she got her magic back, he fell fast asleep.

CIARAN AWOKE IN THE WAGON —BUT HIS HANDS and ankles were tied together with a leather cord that tied him to all the other people in the wagon, including Nadia, who had been moved away from him. That broth had come from Sorcha, so he hadn't questioned it, but where would she have gotten it? Tahra was clever, and he would do well to remember that. She had put something in the broth to make them all sleep.

Nadia was safe, only just waking up as well, bound hand and foot but unmarked and no distress on her face. But her eyes grew wide, and she looked over toward the end of the wagon.

He followed her gaze. The wagon was inside another one of those sacred groves, this one inside the Faerie Wood.

Tahra was already performing her ritual. Eyes closed and moving about in circles with her hands moving up and down, she half sang, half chanted all the while, asking the fae to return her magical powers.

It was now or never.

He glanced around to see what he was up against. The dozen Cameron warriors waited nearby on horseback, their weapons undrawn but at the ready, their horses fidgeting about in the way steeds do when their riders are ready for battle. Ruadh was among them, and he looked the other way whenever 'Bixby' looked at him.

Tahra stopped her dance and turned to look

straight at Ciaran, with recognition. She knew full well who he was, likely had the whole time. Her gesture took in the whole wagonful of people. "Glory tae the Fae! I offer ye this fine batch o' flesh as a sacrifice, in exchange for the return o' my magic. Take them, be glad, and show me yer gratitude." Looking at Ciaran with haughty derision, she raised her hand to signal the warriors.

The Cameron warriors charged through the trees on horses with manes and tails flying, drawing their swords and making dirt clods fly.

With the certainty of his immediate death in his mind, Ciaran grasped the halberd tightly and wished toward it.

Strength drained from him, but as he had wished, all the leather in the area dissolved. The leather that bound him and the others. Everyone's belts and scabbards. Every saddle on every horse. And Tahra's leather hair band.

Tahra's hair fell down, and the wind blew it in her face, making her movements unsure.

The men all fell from their mounts, calling out in the agony of feeling their limbs broken from crashing into the trees. Horses skittered and reared. Terrified by the unexpected feel of losing their riders, they trampled them.

Ciaran frantically gestured toward the back of the wagon, gently urging everyone out. "Run for yer lives. Run. Dinna stop until ye canna gae any farther."

Nadia was scurrying around in the bed of the wagon.

Ciaran turned to urge her out as well, but when he saw what she was after, he stayed to help, kneeling by her side in the wagon bed and grabbing the hundreds of papers which threatened to blow away on the faerie wind. The history book with his name in it had been leather bound, the book they had risked so much to obtain.

Nadia was certain these papers contained the secret to breaking the halberd's curse on him. His name was on these papers, and they were magical, from what little Kelsey had told them. She stuffed them all down the front of her dress.

Ciaran saw one of the Cameron horses nearby and called it over by clicking his tongue against the roof of his mouth.

It came to him readily, lowering its head for Bixby's customary neck pat.

He steadied it with a hand on its soft nose.

Nadia got on bareback, then pled with her eyes for him to get on with her and ride away.

But Tahra was still a threat. She had been momentarily confused by the chaos of all the frantic horses and screaming warriors, but she now resumed her ritual. And the fae could grab the fleeing servants even as they ran, if their desire was made strong enough by the druid child's song.

Un-disguising the halberd to make it more terri-fying, Ciaran charged the druid child, raising the war axe up in the air to smite her head and cleave her clean in two, roaring with all the aggression he had kept inside all these days in the Cameron fortress.

But Tahra drew her sword and took her battle stance.

How had he forgotten sword-fighting with her before? And this time, he didn't have Meehall and Baltair to help him. But his weapon was superior. It had much more reach. He lowered the blow that should have ended the druid child's life.

Tahra fell to the ground an instant before he made contact. She rolled toward him, knocked his feet from under him, and sliced the flesh between his boot and his knee.

Screaming in anguish, he felt her grab the halberd.

He felt the halberd choose the druid child over him.

Felt the cursed weapon leave his hand and leap into Tahra's hand.

Needing to keep the druid child's attention on him so that she didn't turn on Nadia, Ciaran hollered in pain while grabbing his injury, then rolled away from Tahra, cursing the cursed weapon.

❧ 19 ❧

Nadia nearly fell off the gentled horse when she saw Tahra grab the halberd out of Ciaran's limp fingers. But then she saw his chest moving, and her heart beat once more. He was alive. If she could just get him up on this horse with her, she was pretty sure she could get them back to Eoin's tree.

The Druid child stared aghast at the powerful magic weapon in her hands, probably communing with the cursed thing.

Nadia had to move now, before Tahra left this halberd-induced trance. Stealing glances at Tahra, Nadia used a small amount of leg pressure to coax the horse through the green trees of the sacred grove.

She went around the broken bodies of the fallen Cameron warriors to where Ciaran lay.

Oh good. He was but knocked out. There was no blood. None of his limbs were positioned at impossible angles. She could see his chest rise and fall with his breath. Aye, he would recover. She just needed to—

Oh no.

A pleased wicked smile spread across Tahra's face, and the druid child changed her tune. No longer singing to the faeries, Tahra now crooned to the halberd. "Och, sae many o' ye. Aye, I ken ye are the lost souls o' Druids imprisoned by this here halberd. Release ye? Mayhap, but first, as ye are, ye can summon the magic for me. Fortify me. Give me strength. Let me work the magic once more..."

Terrified that Tahra would wish the halberd's magic onto her, Ciaran, or any of her fleeing friends, Nadia did the only thing she could think to do. Squeezing the horse as hard as she could with her legs, she urged him on with her voice while holding onto his mane for dear life and charged him straight at Tahra, hoping he would trample her and put an end to the druid child.

But Tahra brandished the halberd in front of her. A wicked gleam in her eye told Nadia the druid child knew full well what that evil conduit to the afterlife could do and was about to unleash that force. Nadia's only consolation was the shock she saw on Tahra's face when the halberd drained energy from her in order to power whatever spell now lashed out in Nadia's direction.

Nadia's life flashed before her eyes. How had her desire to see the Highlands of Scotland come to death at the hands of a madwoman?

She saw herself studying her Gaelic so hard in school, with a mind only to come and work at the prestigious Celtic University. All the parties she had missed and heard about the next day haunted her. Likewise, the dances and the plays she hadn't attended, but had seen photos and reviews of later, so intent had she been to be chosen by Celtic, to be worthy of Celtic. Several guys had asked her on dates, and granted, she hadn't really been interested, but she now wondered if...

She might've had so much fun in her life, had she not been so intent on what she had thought would be adventure, excitement, and beauty.

Aye, the Highlands were beautiful, but they were so much more so out here in the wild than at Celtic. She could have enjoyed them without going to Celtic. She might have just come to Scotland on vacation, gotten a job anywhere else but at Celtic, and applied for a work visa so she could stay.

Why had she been so intent on the acclaimed institution that she only later found out was run by druids? What had possessed her to waste her youth on studying?

Paralysis hit her, making her fall off the horse.

She landed in the soft green grass. But although she knew nothing was injured, she had to wait there, able only to breathe and think, completely paralyzed by the halberd's magic.

Out of the corner of her eye, she could see Ciaran crawling toward her. She wanted to cry, to cling to him and beg him not to leave her. She knew he would do as she asked, and it was so tempting. More tempting than anything else in her life had ever been.

But when he got close enough, she urged him with her eyes, "Save yerself. Flee from here. I canna move. I am done for, but ye hae a chance. Take it. Dinna let her kill us both with one swing o' that cursed weapon!"

He didn't budge. If anything, he drew closer to her, taking her hand in his.

She had done what she could. His love, pure and strong, was a balm to her despair. She relaxed into it, letting it soothe her last moments with the bliss of being close to him.

But then his eyes grew wide, and she looked where he was looking.

Eoin burst through the woods with Baltair and two extra horses, riding toward them.

The paralysis spell had drained the druid child, but she was still fierce with a weapon. She ran toward Nadia and Ciaran.

Before Tahra got close enough to attack, Eoin took Baltair's hand, leaned down and grabbed Ciaran's other hand, closed his eyes, and concentrated.

The four of them whirled into the dark night street at Celtic University. Eoin and Baltair were still on their horses, but Nadia and Ciaran arrived sitting on the ground. The paved street was cold in a way the dirt had not been.

Nadia waited a few moments for Ciaran to say something to his cousin, but when he didn't, she stepped in. "Thank you for coming to the rescue," he told Eoin sincerely, only swallowing once at how difficult it was to be indebted to him.

Ciaran still didn't say anything, and it was only then she remembered how severely he had been injured. Tears sprang to her eyes when she saw the blood oozing from his leg under his kilt. Her first-aid training kicked in, and she put both hands on the wound, pushing down to staunch the flow of blood.

Eoin dismounted, knelt beside Ciaran, and dug something out of his sporran, which he handed to Ciaran in the way one might hand aspirin to someone. "These are some of Meehall's pills," he told his cousin.

The light returned to Ciaran's eyes, and he took the pills and swallowed them dry.

Baltair was at his side now holding up a water skin for Ciaran to drink, which he did.

Nadia felt left out. "What did you give him?"

Eoin turned a serious face to her. "Is there a place we can store these horses where they won't be so obvious, and another place where he might spend the night and not be noticed?"

Amazed to see Ciaran's wound closing and him getting up, Nadia helped him to his feet and stood, too. "We can stable them with the trail horses. Come, it's not far." She kept ahold of Ciaran's hand and felt his grip grow stronger by the second.

He squeezed her hand, gently but with confidence. "Sarah's man Meehall gave his brother a few o' these pills before he ran off with his new wife tae Murray Castle. The druids made them, but 'tis glad I am for them anyway." He still limped, but that flirtatious gleam was back in his eye, and his face no longer contorted with pain.

"'Tis glad I am to see you smile," she told him breathlessly as they walked, peering into his face to assure herself he was really smiling at her and not still grimacing in pain. Incredible.

He was, and they gawked at each other the whole way to the stables, where Nadia took advantage of the men's preoccupation with the horses to discreetly text Ellie.

"Are you home?"

"Nadia! Of course I'm home. You're the one out having fun."

"Quick, pull out the hide-a-bed. And clean yourself up. Baltair's here!"

"Squee!"

Eoin addressed Nadia quietly as they walked through the open quad on their way to her and Ellie's dorm. "Where's the book?"

Ciaran clamped down on Nadia's hand with his own, still being gentle but giving a clear warning. They could no longer hear each other's thoughts, but that experience had brought them closer to each other than Nadia had ever felt with anyone, not even her parents.

She gave Ciaran's hand one quick squeeze, to let

him know she understood. The book's loosened pages were scratching her skin beneath her bodice, but she was not to tell Eoin she had them.

Ciaran's hold on her hand relaxed a bit, but it was still tense.

She answered Eoin truthfully, which she instinctively knew was necessary. "The book didn't survive the fight."

Ciaran's hand totally relaxed in hers now, as he joined in on the explanation. "Aye, the halberd dissolved it in the course o' decimating a dozen Cameron warriors who were after oor blood."

Eoin grunted.

Before Nadia let them into her and Ellie's dorm room, she said, "I warn you, Baltair, she's awfully eager to see you."

The man properly smiled at this news, but Eoin was grumpy again once they arrived in the dorm room, spoiling the fun of Ellie and Baltair's reunion. "You're limping on purpose, Ciaran. Quit trying to get attention."

Ciaran shared an eye roll with Nadia over his cousin's grumpiness, flopped onto the middle of the couch bed, and started snoring.

It had been a long day. Nadia decided to change the subject, asking Eoin, "How long do you think we need to stay before Tahra will have left the area and it's safe to go back to 1706?"

"Overnight should do it, but in the morning, I'll go alone and check to make sure."

Nadia forced herself to give him a smile. "I can never thank you enough."

To her surprise, he looked at her just as sincerely, and while he didn't smile, just his sincerity was so shocking that it rendered her speechless for a moment. "Nadia, 'tis I should be thanking you. At great risk to yourself, you went and spied on the Camerons for us. You didn't have to do that. Ciaran would have brought you home at the blink of your eye. You are a brave woman, worthy of him."

Dazed by Eoin's unheard of praise, Nadia looked over to see if his cousin shared his opinion.

But Baltair and Ellie were seated side-by-side on her bed, heads together and having a whisper and laugh conversation that would not be interrupted for quite a while, she could tell.

❧

NADIA AND EOIN EXCHANGED WORRIED GLANCES all morning, but by the time they got to Murray camp, Eoin was sure. "Aye, the pills are working, but ainly sae far. Ciaran's wound has mended, but the limp is na gang away. He canna fight like this."

Eoin's wife ran out to meet him with their children, and other relatives in the clan came forward and gave the men hugs as well. A few gave Ellie and Nadia curious glances, but they were all welcoming.

Ellie spent most of her time with Baltair. There had been no question of leaving Ellie behind. She would not have stood for that. But now they had to go back to Celtic. They needed the reference materials there. Ellie had already told Baltair, but now Nadia had to break the news to Ciaran. It was good news though. He should take it well.

Nadia made herself put on a big smile when she went to go see Ciaran in the tent he shared with Baltair. "Sae who performs weddings in yer clan?" she asked him with a knowing smile that contained all the encouragement she could manage.

He did look pleased, but there was sadness in his face as well, and she couldn't blame him. Except for the last few days when he'd been playing the part of a cripple, all he had ever been was a warrior. He put on a happy face. "There be a kirk na far from here with a priest who can wed folk."

He had stood up when she came in. She went

over, took him in her arms, and kissed him, making it very clear he was the only one for her.

❧

ELLIE HADN'T WANTED TO RETURN TO CELTIC so soon, but Nadia had insisted, saying they had a pressing translation only they could conduct, amid the stacks of ancient texts at the university. So here they were, dropped off in the dark alley of Celtic once more, with the men leaving immediately.

Ellie turned to Nadia and joked, "I know you wanted that promotion, but isn't this taking it a little too far? I mean, you're marrying Ciaran. The whole clan knows it. And Ciaran wants to stay in 1706. Even with a promotion, your job here wouldn't be worth the commute."

Nadia rewarded Ellie with the first smile she had seen on her friend all day.

"There's the spirited woman I know," Ellie told her friend. "So what are we going to tr—"

Nadia put her hand over Ellie's mouth and looked around as if there could be people listening from thin air.

Come to think of it, there probably could be. Who knew what druids were capable of doing with their magic? Ellie took a deep breath and nodded. "OK, I'll keep quiet, but you need to tell me why we came back here. You aren't the only one with a man who will miss her."

Smiling apologetically, Nadia let go of Ellie and got out a small pad of paper and a pencil, then scribbled on it furiously. "We need to keep this from the druids. Especially from Kelsey. She can't know. Tell me you agree. Write it down."

Really?

But the look on Nadia's face brooked no nonsense.

Ellie wrote on the pad, "I promise to keep this from all the druids, especially from Kelsey, at the cost of everything but anyone's life or limb. Now tell me what we rushed away from our men to translate."

The story continues in Baltair – A Time Travel Romance,
by Jane Stain.

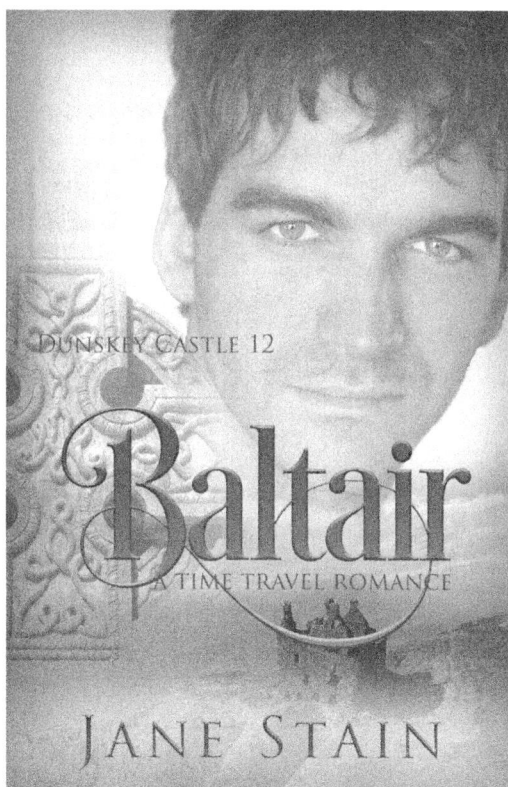

Made in the USA
Las Vegas, NV
02 December 2021

35888725R00125